The Life and Deaths of Carter Falls

Gypsey Teague

PublishAmerica

Baltimore

First printing

ISBN: 1-59286-435-X
PUBLISHED BY PUBLISHAMERICA BOOK
PUBLISHERS
www.publishamerica.com
Baltimore

Printed in the United States of America

With Thanks

First I would like to thank Marla who has lived with me through this process and has kept me sane. She has also been my reader, proofer, and sounding board. You are the love of my life. I would like to thank Fran for her technical expertise in Manchester. It had been a long time since I had been home and streets change. I would like to thank Mindi and Dawn who read the manuscript for flow. And finally I would like to thank the people of Carter Falls who took me into their fold when I was a young tourist and allowed me to write their story.

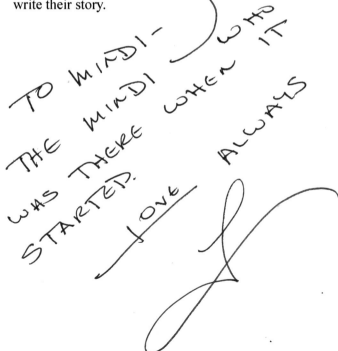

TO MINDI -
THE MINDI
WAS THERE WHEN IT
STARTED.

LOVE

ALWAYS

PROLOG

2100 hours, September 9th, 2000
Taiwan Embassy, Washington, D. C.

The guests and dignitaries of Washington were there. The Taiwanese Embassy was having its' Fall Night of the Dragon. On this night the Chinese look forward to the fall crops with exuberance and gusto. Every director from every intelligence agency in Washington was there in addition to at least one representative of every major foreign governmental agency.

Although the two Americans that walked through the great hall looked like twins, they were actually cousins. The two invited guests, Danny St. Claire and Claire Daniels, were representatives of the National Security Agency, on loan to the State Department. They were there for eye candy. Danny was tall, thin with broad shoulders, bright blue eyes, and deep red hair. His cousin Claire was taller, with equally broad shoulders, and, what some would say, too much chest for her frame. With a thin waist and full hips, her hair brushed back from her face and to her shoulders, she could have modeled or wrestled, and done either exceptionally well.

By ten o'clock they had made the rounds of the party and were standing outside on the portico talking to some friends from main land China. A lone waiter with a tray of soiled napkins was making his way from the great hall to the kitchen when he dropped the tray behind the group. Spinning around quickly at the noise agent St. Claire saw, and reacted too slowly to stop, what was happening. The waiter grabbed a machine pistol with his left hand and began firing. Three rounds struck Danny in the chest; one entered Claire's back, exited her front, and entered the wife of the Deputy of Foreign Culture across the table. Two bodyguards, the Deputy of Foreign Culture, his wife, the Assistant Director of Food Reserves and his wife were all killed. Seven other guests were injured. Surprisingly enough the waiter walked into the kitchen during the panic and walked out the back door to a waiting car in the alley. As the first ambulance pulled up at the front gate, the waiter was sitting across town having a late dinner.

2340 hours, September 9th, 2000
Bethesda Navel Hospital, Bethesda, Maryland

"We have two coming in, one DOA." The doctor on duty called for nurses in the emergency room. "I need blood cross matched and an o.r. opened immediately."

The bleeding agent on the paramedic's gurney was male, red headed, and breathing with the help of a respirator. Three bullets were in his chest; two puncturing his left lung, one lodged less than an inch from his heart.

"Get me a spreader kit and let's get him into o.r."

Five hours later Danny St. Claire lay in intensive care, tubes and wires attached to every clear spot on his body. The bullets had been removed, but his chances of recovery were still slim.

Standing in the shadows of the room were two complete strangers to Danny and to themselves. One was a very tall man in a tuxedo and muddy shoes. The other was a black woman in black jogging shorts, a black sports bra, black fanny pack, and black running shoes. Only her socks had color, and they were international orange.

CHAPTER ONE

1400 hours, May 7, 2001
St. Anthony's Hospital
Nashua, New Hampshire

Morphine is a wonderful drug. When you get it you drift off almost immediately and when they wake you you don't really know how long you were out. The pretty red head in post op was at that stage. She was aware that she was not home; she knew that she had had surgery; she even knew that there were others in the room, but they were just blurred faces, slowly coming into focus.

"How long will she be out?" A tall man in gray slacks and a short sleeve button down shirt asked the physician standing by the bed.

"She should be aware of her surroundings in about an hour." The doctor picked up his clipboard and walked out of the room. "Since you're going to be here until she wakes I'll leave you to it. Call me if you need anything. The nurse will be in in a few minutes to check on her pulse." And with that he left.

The third person still in the room, standing next to the tall man was a black woman in her thirties. Poised, agile, and with a sense of spring steel in her stance she stood five foot six, and weighed about one hundred twenty five pounds. If there was any wasted skin or fat on her it was lost to sight. Her hair was long, straight, and tied back, her shoulders erect, her breasts were full and round, her hips showing no sign of children. Neatly tucked into the waistband of her Chloe skirt was a Glock 9 mm and two spare clips. Doctor Rachel Jackson was not just a pretty face.

"Sir, do you think she'll be all right now?" Rachel looked at the tall man.

"At lot has happened in the last six months. It hasn't been easy for any of us. I think the situation will resolve itself with time and energy. Claire will be a viable part of the Agency again within the year if she's allowed to heal on her own, with some help."

"So it's still your plan to let her recuperate in Carter Falls?"

"Can you think of a better place than her childhood playground? It was a place where she felt safe and secure, with no one shooting her or trying to kill everyone around her? I think the situation warrants the time, yes."

The tall man turned to look at the woman in the bed. He saw an attractive red head, although the hair was pulled back away from her pale face. From under the covers she appeared to be about five foot eight, one hundred and forty pounds, a little heavy in the thighs from years of bike racing. Her breathing revealed large breasts, evenly spaced against her ribs. Her hands, and one was attached to a monitor, were neither rough nor smooth. The years of fieldwork for the agency had taken their toll. A manicure would do wonders, but the woman in the bed would wrinkle her nose at such feminine things. As he turned away the woman's eyes opened briefly and she tried to speak.

Rachel walked over to the bed and whispered into her ear.

"Claire, it's Rachel. You're going to be all right. Just rest a few more minutes and then the anesthesia will wear off.

"The woman looked up with glazed eyes and said "I'm not Claire, I'm Danny" and then fell back asleep.

Two hours later Claire Daniels was awake and smiling. Her surgery, which was a breast augmentation, went well and she was getting ready to be checked out. The tall man had left once secure in the fact that Claire was able to leave. He showed little outward concern for one of his best agents, but he was relieved that the last of the medical corrections were completed. Claire had been through a lot in the past six months; shot three times by one of her closest friends, her cousin killed in the same barrage, her brush with death and the recovery of the injuries. Finally reconstruction surgery to enhance her breasts as a psychological operation to make her feel better, but all the time with three round white scars across her upper chest, one missing her heart by less than an inch, the others puncturing her left lung.

"I can walk on my own, *thank you*," Rachel heard before she saw the ruckus Claire was causing.

Claire had been told she had to be taken by wheel chair to the front doors before discharge. Now Claire was standing in front of the chair, wearing her hair loose and matted about her face, her blouse with one button done, over a tight sports bra to hold in the day surgery of implants, her skirt skewed to one side, and wearing one sandal.

"Sure Claire," said Rachel helping her friend into the chair, "you are such a big girl. You can even dress yourself without help. NOT!"

At that the two of them began laughing until sharp pain under her rib cage caused the red head in the wheel chair to take a deep breath of air.

"Okay, lead me out of here before they stick something else in me."

The drive back to Manchester from Nashua was uneventful. Claire slept most of the way. Between the drugs at the hospital and the Darvocet for the pain she was pretty much beat. Rachel, however, kept track of the traffic and the black SUV that kept a safe distance behind them, with four special agents inside, to make certain that the Lexus reached the safe house. Claire Daniels was an intricate part of a much greater plan, and nothing was going to go wrong on their watch.

"Hey, sleepy, wake up." Rachel reached over and tapped Claire's shoulder as the Lexus pulled into the condo parking lot. "Time to go to bed."

"What?" Claire looked out the window. "It's dark out."

The car parked under the building and Rachel helped Claire out of the car. The two women entered the elevator and exited on the fourth floor onto the deep green pile carpet of the hall. The old mills that the condos had been renovated from dated back to the early 1800's. At times there had been tanneries, gun powder manufacturers, a company that made steam engines for trains, and a hat embroidery shop. Now it housed very select condominiums of the rich and famous, that wanted to have a look at the Merrimac River and the older part of the city.

'I'm hungry," said Claire, heading for the fridge. "Did you get the fruit?"

Grabbing a bag of cherries she gently sat on an overstuffed chair and let out a deep breath.

"This has been a hell of a day." Rachel said, sitting across from her and sipping a white wine cooler.

"You should have had the day I had." Returned Claire. "Wake up as one person go to bed as another, and a dead one at that." She gave a strange look at her friend and got up quickly. "Shit I forgot." Moving as fast as she could to the bathroom she leaned over and threw up.

Rachel ran up behind her to steady her. "Are you all right?"

Claire slumped to the floor with her head hanging over the toilet. She began to cry between spasms of retching.

"How did I get to this?" She cried. "I was happy, I liked myself, I had a good job, my truck ran, my car turned heads, I could piss standing up without people looking into the stall to see who was there. I didn't care what I looked like. I wasn't a dead woman. Now I can't even bend forward without falling over from the weight. I'm Danny. Is it so hard to tell?" Claire looked up with tears on both cheeks, rolled her eyes and passed out.

Rachel dragged her friend to her bed, propped her on it and rolled her over. Slowly so as not to rip the sutures she undressed the red head, put on a pink flannel nightgown and tucked her in. She knew that she would catch hell in the morning for the nightgown in pink but she didn't care.

Rachel went back to the living room and poured another glass of wine. Claire was right, she had had a worse day than one could imagine. When Rachel had been assigned this case as the psychological assessment officer she wondered what it would be like. A male agent that was basically ordered to undergo gender reassignment; up to but not including his genitals. How could she put herself in Claire's position? Two days after Danny was shot the agency was already planning the cross over. He was told that it was necessary for his safety, that the shooter had been after him and not his cousin, but she wondered if it had been the best choice at the time. To undergo the intense hormonal therapy was traumatic enough, but to be forced to undergo it when it was not your original idea must have been hell. Finally to take the identity of the one individual that was closest to him in all his life must have killed him internally. The next six months would decide whether Danny St. Claire would remain an agent or not. It might even decide if Danny would remain sane.

May 8, 2001
Safehouse
Manchester, New Hampshire

Spring in New Hampshire is a beautiful thing. The air is crisp with still cool breezes. The snow, at least what is left, is a reminder that the winters are hard, and summer is fleeting, but when the sun rises and the birds begin to sing, you don't care. Add to that the view from the mill yards and Manchester can sometimes be called inspiring. Claire woke up a little after nine, hungry, dirty, sore and confused. She lay in bed a few minutes with the nightgown around her waist; Danny slept nude, and listened to the traffic. She and her cousin grew up in this town, but even this was foreign now.

Remembering to move slowly she walked to the bathroom and without looking at the mirror started a bath. With slow movements she took off the nightgown and the sports bra. At one point under her left arm the blood stuck to the skin and the cloth and pulled a little. Finally she got it over her head and sat on the toilet to pee. When she began taking over Claire's identity there was a professional drag performer that was called in to give Danny some suggestions. One hint was that even if you can pee standing up, don't. Learn to do everything as a woman would, mentally in time it will take hold and become second nature. In the beginning it was hard. More than once a woman would scream at the hospital or training center because the shorthaired lady in the stall next to her was peeing standing up. Finally it took.

Rachel was at the door by the time Claire eased into the tub. "I thought I heard you get up." She looked down her friend. "Are you hungry or are you going to throw it up again?"

Claire looked up through the steam and gave a little smile.

"I think it's only the night of the morphine." Claire dunked her head in the water and rose up. "I had morphine once when I had knee surgery. The nurse said that comfort food was always good after surgery so on the way home I had chocolate covered orange peels and a can of Moxie. What the nurse didn't say was sugar and morphine don't mix. Ten minutes later my dad's Buick was covered with bits of chocolate, orange peels and smelled like Moxie. I swore I would never forget that." She began to wash her hair. "So much for memory."

"How bout eggs?" Rachel headed for the door.

"Hey did they do something funny to my hair?" Claire shouted after Rachel left.

A few minutes later her hair in a towel, her face cleaned, a new bra and panties on and a black Victoria Secrets robe over that, a much more contented Claire Daniels entered the living room and finally the kitchen.

"Did you say something about your hair?" Rachel began scooping scrambled eggs and bacon onto two plates at the bar.

"Claire sat down, took off the towel and pulled slightly at her hair. "Yea, this" meaning her hair, "wasn't this long yesterday."

Rachel sat on her bar stool. "While you were under they had extensions put in to make your hair the same lengths as Claire. HE figured the closest they could get to Claire the better for your safety. "What do you think?"

"About the hair or the eggs?" Claire finished the last piece of bacon and put the dish in the dishwasher.

"Both, either, pick one."

"The eggs were a little runny, but the bacon was good." Claire went to the living room. "The hair is a perfect match to Claire's'. When I looked in the mirror it really did look like I was across from her picture."

Rachel sat on the couch across from Claire.

"Are you well enough to talk a little." Rachel took out a small recorder and placed it between the women on the coffee table. "I'm supposed to do an evaluation as soon after the surgery as possible."

"God you never quit." Claire got up and walked around the room. "I can't even sneeze without someone asking if it's part of the grieving process, am I going through survivors guilt, do I feel like killing myself." Her tone softened when she saw that Rachel was really concerned, and not just doing this as part of her job. "I'm sorry, but this is all I've been given for six months."

"If you don't want to talk, that's okay too." Rachel shut off the recorder. "But there are some issues that we should talk about, either way. You're the only one who can tell me what is going on in your head. I can't even imagine what it's been like. Hell I'd be a basket case by now if it where me."

Claire went to the bathroom and came back with her hairbrush. She walked over to the recorder, picked it up, rewound the tape, turned it on and put it on the table. Sitting back in her chair she began brushing her hair.

"I'll start at the beginning, in case the agency decided to skip something." She leaned over to the table and spoke very deliberately. "This is the only time I will tell this story so whoever is listening to this, get it right the first time." Sitting back she finished her hair, tossed the brush onto the other occasional chair in the room, looked out the large picture window to a cloudless Spring sky and began talking.

" I was born right here in Manchester of fraternal twin parents. Nowadays I don't know if that's rare, but at that time the chances of two singles of a pair of fraternal twins meeting and producing a child was quite unusual. To add to the mix my cousin Claire Daniels was the product of the other set of each pair. We, however, were not twins since we were cousins. We were born a year apart, but by the time we were five you would swear that we were brother and sister from the same womb.

Our parents lived two doors apart in the suburbs. Not a great town to grow up in, but clean and safe enough for the time. Between our houses was a family by the name of Lavesque. They had a son at the same time Claire was born and the three of us, Claire, Steve, and I played and swam, and partied, and grew up best friends. Through High School we did the normal childhood things, football games, hunting, fishing, camping, we each took some kind of martial art, I ran track, Claire played softball, and Steve pitched baseball.

After High School Steve and I went to the University at Durham. Claire went to Keene State, farther south. Even though we each majored in different fields, with different languages we were still inseparable. I expected Steve to marry Claire after graduation, but they never really clicked. I guess she was just too stubborn or he was just too wild. In the summer of 82 we decided to do something crazy and we enlisted in the Army. The recruiter was a friend of ours from High School and promised we would stay together after basic training.

In the second week at Fort Benning we were recruited for Officer Candidate School, because of our four-year college degrees. Looking back I should have run out of that office screaming, finished my three years and come back home, instead we all said "hell yea" and went to the Benning School for Boys, and now Girls. We were in school for two years after that. OCS, Military Intelligence Officer Basic School, Airborne, again because we thought that it would be a kick, Ranger School for Steve and I, they still didn't let girls into that one; Claire went to demolition school at Ft Bragg, instead, Language School at the Defense Language Institute at Presidio of Monterey, and finally the Q School at Quantico with the Central and Defense Intelligence Agencies. Steve became a sniper as well as his team leader. He said it increased his kill ratio.

For three years after that we traveled the world with our respective teams, correcting the mistakes of other agencies and agents. One week in East Berlin, the next in Taiwan, two days home to Fort Ord for debriefing and back again. My team lost sixteen of the thirty-four members by the time we retired it. Claire lost almost that many and Steve lost over twenty in the same time period. His last mission before disbandment was supposed to be an easy extraction in Bosnia.

The contact came back, he didn't. Claire cried for days and I felt as if I had lost a brother. That was seventeen years ago.

After that Claire and I joined the desk set at the National Security Agency. I tracked arms sales in the Far East and she worked the European desk. Life became routine, neither of us married; we stayed in constant touch, lived close and worked too much. From time to time a note would pass by one of our desks indicating that someone or some group had died unexpectedly with no leads. Over the years the clues led to one individual; a white male, often described as missing his right index finger. It wasn't until last year that we finally got a photo of the individual: It was Steve Levesque. He was older and more tanned but it was Steve. Somehow he had not died in Bosnia and had become a free agent.

From that day on we formed a task force to find him and put him out of business. He, on the other hand did everything he could to stay as active as possible; tied to two political assassinations, one terrorist bombing, the Al Queda, the Hamas, and even being paid as a double agent for the Mossad.

Six months ago Claire and I were at an embassy party for the Taiwan Ambassador. We were out on the portico talking to some Chinese Nationals when a waiter behind us dropped a tray. I turned quickly and saw Steve holding an Uzi machine pistol. That was the last thing I remembered until I woke up at Bethesda two days later. The doctors took three bullets out of my chest, one just missing my heart. Claire was not as lucky. She had been hit with one round through her back and passing through her heart. Five others died and seven were injured. Operations said I had been the target since I was the leader of the task force. Somehow Steve found out about the Embassy party and arranged to be there. To throw Steve off the track while I was still in surgery the news reported that I had been killed and that Claire had survived. The agency brought in the tall man to handle the recovery operation and he came up with the idea that I become Claire. He thought that since we looked like twins, and we had the same memories of Steve I could best handle the investigation without any loss of progress. I did not realize that I would have had

15

to go into protection without this scheme, but to become Claire was not something that I had ever considered, nor at the time did I fully understand what it involved. You probably know the rest from the files. First there was the hormone injections, the electrolysis, the exercise, the diet, the voice coach, the clothes, the mannerisms, which were second nature quickly due to our closeness, and finally the cosmetic surgery. When this is all over the agency has said that I will be returned to normal and will continue my work as Danny St. Claire, but for now I'm Claire Daniels, dead agent in disguise."

By the time the tape ran out it was noon. The two women had been at the session for two hours and were both tired. Claire went to take a nap and Rachel went to the computer to type up her notes. She felt as if she were betraying a friend by reporting on what she had just heard but her job was to assess the mental condition of this agent, even if she was becoming a close friend. *She*. Did this word even apply here? One minute Claire is talking about being Danny and knowing Claire, the next he is talking about being Claire and Danny is in the background. He and she were being exchanged at light speed.

She made a sandwich and a cup of tea. Sitting in the kitchen she called the tall man.

The phone picked up on the first ring and she made it short.

"I think there is some damage to the personality. I don't know if this was the right choice in this matter, but we're stuck with it." Listening for a few seconds she continued. "Yes I know I said it would work, but there is more proximity than I expected. I've never seen two people that were closer and not identical siblings. Yes, yes, no I don't think it's too early to make a decision. Yes, probably a couple of days. Yes I will. If you think that you can do it yourself." At that she hung up the phone.

Claire slept until four that afternoon. When she finally came out of her room she was in a denim jumper and maroon sweater. Her red hair was tucked behind each ear with a few wisps of bang loose. The clouds that had been in her eyes seemed to be lifting and they were as blue as they always had been. She even had lipstick on, but at that she drew the line for makeup.

"I have shrimp stir fry for supper." Rachel called from the kitchen. "Do you want a salad with that or just fruit?"

"I'll just have the stir fry." Claire grabbed a Moxie out of the fridge.

"How can you drink that crap?" Rachel curled her nose and sipped a Diet Coke.

"Raised on it." Claire gave her deepest Nor' Eastern accent. "Don't matter wat it tastes like, just like it."

"Gods how can anyone understand anyone else around here with that accent?" Rachel headed for her room. "I've been in sweats all day, and if you're going to dress for dinner, then woe be it for me to look like a slob."

Claire followed Rachel into the bedroom, plopped on the bed and grabbed a pillow around her breasts.

"Did you call him?" She looked at Rachel.

"You know I did." Rachel stripped and started looking in one of her drawers for underwear.

Claire couldn't help but admire the dark skinned beauty. Tall, firm, with the hardest thighs she had ever seen. Danny would have loved to have known Rachel. She caught the thought too late. Danny would have loved? She was Danny.

Burying the thought she asked. "What did he say?"

"Same stuff we've been hearing all along. How are you? Can you continue the mission? He asked if he needed to come here and do it himself."

"What did you say to that?"

"I told him that if he wanted to do that he could do it on his own." Rachel pulled on a long black dress that looked one step removed from a slip. She braided her long hair in one braid and tied it with a hair cord.

"Can we continue until supper is done?" Rachel walked back into the living room. "I can finish this now and be done with it for some time."

Claire kept the pillow in front of her like a shield and followed her friend into the living room. Back in the same positions as before, the tape running, the psychologist and the patient began again.

"You told me your history," Rachel played with her glass, "now tell me what you think. Ramble if you wish. You've been keeping things bottled up for six months, I want to know what you really think, what really bothers you. What is at your core?" A strong black hand reached over and shut off the tape player. "And this time it's just between us girls."

"Us girls?" Claire looked straight and hard at Rachel. "Listen to how you phrase things. "Just us girls? Did anyone think that I may not want to be just one of the girls? I heard that HE had hormones and chemicals in me before I was out of recovery for the shooting. This was never my idea." She sat back and unbuttoned the jumper. "Did anyone really care if I didn't want to be a woman? Did anyone really listen when I said that Steve could be found if I was used as bait? That it would be cheaper and quicker if I continued my work and watched my back better?" Claire pulled up her sweater, unhooked the front clasp on her bra and pulled it away from her chest.

"Look at this." She pushed her breasts at Rachel across the room. "Stitches under each arm pit, nine pounds of saline in each breast. I can't even bend over without balancing myself so I won't fall. How the hell do fat women even move, if these are normal?" She redressed.

"But they're good looking breasts." Rachel tried to defuse the situation with a little humor, even if it was edgy.

"Fuck you." Claire shouted back. "No wait," she gave a sick little laugh, "I can't do that. I'm Claire. That's something Danny would say."

Running her fingers through her red hair she got up and began pacing again. Danny never paced.

"You want to know how I feel, I feel sick and tired. I've been poked and prodded for six months. I've been cut, injected, filled, spied on, and laughed about. I find out about things when I wake up." Holding her hair forward of her face. "I can't even have a say as to my own hair. I've been two people for too long. I want to be just one person." She sat back down.

They ate in silence. Neither really tasted their shrimp. A lot had passed today and the food was just something to get over with. After supper Claire took a bath and went to bed. Rachel stood by the bedroom door for a while after Claire closed it and heard the crying. It would do her good, she thought, to get that out of her system. Danny would never have allowed himself to cry. At least now as Claire she could show some emotions.

It was after midnight when Rachel finally fell asleep. She was worried about her friend. She didn't know what HE would do if this didn't work. She wondered if another problem resolution team was already getting a folder on the two of them.

CHAPTER TWO

0800 hours, May 9, 2001
Manchester, New Hampshire

The shift change for the security went off without incident. The night shift, who Claire called Mack and Myer, after an old television pair of comedians of the sixties, signed the log book and handed it to the day shift, that Rachel called Frick and Frack. Once Mack and Myer were headed back to station for the day, Frick and Frack drove around the corner to the parking lot and ran a sweep of the cars.

"Base, this is Burns." Frick said into his lapel piece. "We have activity at the Lexus."

Burns got out of the SUV, pistol in hand, and approached the parked Lexus.

"I'm approaching the car now. It appears that someone is sitting in the drivers seat, asleep. I am coming around the drivers side now."

Burns walked up even to the driver's window and looked in.

"Base this is Burns, the occupant appears to be male, with shabby clothing, and slumped over the wheel. Am activating the automatic door opener now."

As soon and the door swung open the occupant fell sideways and slumped out of the car, his left hand striking the pavement. He was buckled into the seat and only his upper torso moved.

"Base this is Burns, the occupant is dead. I say again the occupant is dead."

"Base this is Dougherty," Frack broke in, "I just saw a light on at the safe house. I say again we have activity in the safe house."

Within four minutes an identical Lexus 300 was parked under the building in the assigned space. The body and the bloodied car were on their way to the labs in Boston. Not even Jackson or Daniels would know the difference between the two cars.

Claire was up before Rachel. She took a long bath, washed and conditioned her hair and shaved her legs. From time to time she still marveled how much work went into being a woman. The cosmetics and soaps alone could break a small countries economy. The bags under her eyes from crying herself to sleep were not as bad as she thought after the bath. A little makeup and they covered up quite well. Stretching slightly she felt better from the surgery. The doctors said that she should have a full range of motion in a week or so, but at least today she could scratch her back without pulling her front.

Since she was only an inch shorter than the original Claire, the agency never bought her new clothes. After Claire's death they just put everything in boxes and stored it until it was needed. The day before the surgery the same agents moved enough into the safe house to get her by for a week. The rest they took to the Carter Falls house. Likewise Danny's clothing was stored away, along with his personal items, until they were needed. Over the last six months Claire had gotten a crash course in clothes. She could identify Chloe from Vera Wang. She new the right Fendi shoes and bags, the correct length of Pashmina, and where it was still worn, and which perfume went where.

The thermometer outside her window showed fifty-three degrees. Not bad for the first week of May. She guessed by the smell in the air it would not rain until after dark, and should reach almost sixty degrees by three. Now came the fun part; dressing up. Women might spend a fortune on clothes but in the right outfit you felt like you owned the world. When she was Danny she grabbed whatever was handy and clean and threw it on. Now she wouldn't dare wear the wrong dress. Black under wire bra was the first thing on. Claire had been a big girl. She was stocky but not masculine. Her shoulders were wide and her breasts had been DD on a thirty-eight inch rib cage. Claire regretted, feeling the weight on her shoulder straps, that her cousin had not been petite and smaller chested like Rachel.

Next came a black pair of Haynes for Women, a dark gray cargo skirt by McCartney, a steel blue turtleneck sweater she found in the closet with no label, and four inch chunky heel knee high boots in black leather. In front of her mirror she chose a muted red lip stick and put on some base. Finally eye shadow and a scarf for her hair when she left and she was ready for the world.

Walking past Rachel's room and seeing the rest of the house still without activity she pounded on the door.

"Hey, rise and shine. I'm buying breakfast when you're ready." Claire was already past the door and into the living room by the time she finished talking.

Rachel poked her head out the door and yawned. "Who stuck Cheerios in your crotch?"

"It's going to be a pretty day, I feel like driving, I'm really hungry this time, and I forgive you for being a shit yesterday. Let's go out." Claire looked out over the mills.

The condo was on the corner and had a view of three sides of the city. To the south was the Amoskeag Street Bridge, which crossed the Merrimac River from the south end of Elm Street to Second Street. Looking east you could see the city proper. When he was a kid there was always activity downtown. Then the Bedford Mall came in the sixties, then the Mall of New Hampshire in the seventies and the downtown dried up. He remembered the night that Moreau's Lumberyard burned to the ground. From his grandparent's living room, high on Holly Ave, the fire lit up the sky. The paint department had caught fire and that was all it took. Now it was an empty parking lot just across the canal. It was sort of representative of the entire area, things close and people move. Finally looking west was the river. Growing up the river was often six inches deep in blood. The slaughterhouses under the bridge would dump the refuse straight into the river. Claire remembered her senior summer from High School, working nights with Steve at the tannery just down the block and shooting rats at lunch break; a lawyer's high-rise apartment occupies the space today. Now the water was crystal clean and trout swam up stream. By the time she was done reminiscing Rachel was standing next to her looking out the same window.

Rachel had chosen conservatively. Wool slacks and a silk blouse with jacket, she had a matching necklace and earrings of gold filigree. Her hair was again braided and tied; held on the top of her head with a pair of gold hairpins.

"What's on the agenda today?" Rachel, wearing flats, looked up at Claire, at least six inches taller in boots.

"Today, my friend I show you my home town."

With that the red head grabbed her friend by the arm and literally lifted her out of the apartment.

Once in the elevator, and going to the basement, Claire began talking. When Claire was excited, Rachel usually had a hard time understanding every word. Rachel came from the upper middle class of Maryland. Claire was from Yankee country, as the agency used to say. A Yankee accent was sometimes so thick that it was another language. Today seemed to be one of those times. Rachel readied herself for a long day.

" I know this great place for breakfast." Claire walked into the parking garage ahead of her friend. "It has the least healthy eggs and bacon on the planet, but you die happy."

"Yea, but remember girl friend, you ain't got that metabolism to lose the calories, anymore." Rachel put everything she had into a lower east side ethnic twang. "You gonna look like fat mammas ass when you done."

"Nope," Claire headed for a dark corner of the garage, " I also know where we're going for lunch, and then salad for supper."

With Frick and Frack safely on the other side of the lot, Claire reached a car mitten covering something very low to the ground. She hit a switch on her key chain and the locks holding it in place slipped free, pulled off the mitten and stood back with a great grin on her face.

"What the hell is this?" Rachel almost sat on the concrete from shock. "And when did you park it here?"

The two women stared at the metallic blue, 1974 Porsche 914 S for a few minutes then Claire opened the trunk and shoved the cover in it.

"I parked it here about two weeks ago. You didn't think I'd be seen driving in a Lexus all summer did you?" Claire opened the driver's door and got in. "Get your butt in the seat, woman, and let's go eat."

The Porsche fired immediately and almost purred with vibrations. Claire had backed the car into the space so when she put it in gear and hit the gas it shot out of the lot like a sprinter out of the blocks. The car was across the canal bridge before the agency SUV could start their vehicle.

"You better slow down a little so Frick and Frack can follow." Rachel quipped. "If not they'll have every cop in town out looking for us."

"Yea I guess you're right. Can't be that obvious with blue and red lights all around us." At the next stoplight she pulled over and waited for the black SUV. It took almost three minutes for the vehicle to pull up behind them, and with a wave the girls were off again.

"How did you get the car to the safe house?" Rachel looked at the city as they drove by. Manchester must have been a great place once. The majestic buildings on either side of Elm Street, the main thoroughfare, were at least a hundred, if not two hundred years old. The granite facades were stunning. Rachel had never been one to admire architecture, but she was beginning to understand why some people spent their lives studying the ancient buildings of Europe.

"When Claire was killed the car was in Oklahoma having the engine rebuilt. There's a guy in OKC that is a god," Claire threw up her hands in mock adoration, "with Porsches. He kept the car and shipped it after I got better. When I heard HIM say I was going to the safe house in Manchester, I had the garage send it there. Two weeks ago it was delivered and I mittened it in Kevlar and waited." Claire pulled into a small shopping center off the main street and shut down the engine. "Claire and I built this from the ground up. It was more her car than mine, I still love the Brits, but we worked on each equally. The flaring over the wheels adds to the draft. The engine is six cylinders, two liter, air, and forced oil cooled with fuel injection. It gets thirty two miles to the gallon at ninety miles an hour and will bury the needle."

Rachel looked at the speedometer and noted it said one hundred sixty miles per hour. She shuddered a little to think of that speed, so close to the ground.

"The color," Claire continued, "was a compromise between black and silver. We settled on metallic blue with twenty layers of hand rubbed clear lacquer. It never needs polish, just a light wash cloth."

The greasy spoon turned out to be an old Waffle House. It was now called Frida's Fabulous Fritters. Claire said that Frida had been the owner's dog when they opened. Now three brothers ran it and the food just kept getting better. The two girls had eggs, bacon, toast, coffee, tea, orange juice, and waffles. By eleven o'clock they were full and ready to shop.

"Now," As Claire roared out of the parking lot and headed east, "we go to the Mall."

Claire pulled onto Beech Street and headed south and then onto South Willow Street.

"When I was a kid this was all empty. There used to be a drive in there," she pointed to a Bradlees', now closed, "and there was a pond behind it that we could fish in. Now it's just one building after another."

Once in the Mall of New Hampshire Claire studied the You Are Here sign for a few minutes and then struck off down the boulevard.

"This morning I decided to do something I have never done before." Rachel began to worry. "Today I'm having my nails done."

For the next hour Rachel, Claire, and the two nail techs talked about everything. They talked about cars, clothes, food, men; a subject that Rachel found interesting because Claire spoke as though she had been a woman all her life, and women. Then they went to every clothing store in the Mall and bought clothes. Rachel tried to make mental notes about Claire's actions, but gave up. Claire was on a planet all her own today and there was no rhyme or reason to it.

By three the two were tired, hungry, and had spent quite a bit of the agencies money. 'It's only money, and not mine.' Claire said more than once. 'If HE is going to make me beautiful, then HE is going to pay for it.'

"Now comes the best part of the day. Sushi!"

Rachel almost gagged at the sound of raw fish. She turned around and headed back into the Mall, but Claire was already ahead of her and herding her to the car.

"Come on." Claire chided. "You've faced terrorist, killers, drug dealers, and HIM. How bad can some rice and vegetables be?"

"No raw fish." Rachel stomped her foot on the asphalt.

"Exactly." Claire laughed and the car raced out of the parking lot.

"What happened to you last night?" Rachel asked Claire.

"What do you mean?" Claire turned onto I 93 and headed south.

"Last night you were damned to be unhappy and Claire. Today if I didn't know you I'd swear you'd been born Claire." Rachel watched the cars slip by as the Porsche reached 85 and then 90 miles an hour.

"I woke up this morning and just felt better. Like I had come to some great shibumi, you know, enlightenment. I realized that for whatever reason I was stuck here for the time being and making the most of it just seemed to make sense." Claire started to slow the car down for the Bedford exit. "Is this something that goes into your report?"

"Hell any of this could go into my report." Rachel grabbed for the handhold as the car took the off ramp at sixty. "Does this car ever go slow?"

Claire shot through a yellow light and parked in front of a green door at the back of the Bedford Mall.

"This car has a fifty-one/forty-nine weight distribution. Its taken corners at seventy. The only time you have to worry is when the tires squeal."

"Why?" Rachel got out of the car quickly, before Claire drove to the next state.

"When the tires squeal, the car is about two seconds from rolling. It's one of those car things."

Car things, thought Rachel. Now we're into car things.

NO RAW FISH was the name of the sushi bar. It was a quiet place with shoji rooms and seats in front of the bar where you could watch your sushi and nigiri prepared. Claire ordered for both of them. She had the tuna nigiri, raw tuna on sushi rice, the unagi, broiled eel on sushi rice, and kappa maki, cucumber and rice rolled in seaweed. For Rachel Claire ordered the California roll, which was avocado, cucumber, cooked shrimp, sprouts, and rice rolled in seaweed, and a spring salad of daikon radish and cucumber. Very hot, strong green tea washed to down.

"I was thinking." Claire stuffed a piece of tuna in her mouth. "I'm bored here and need to go home. Tomorrow let's go to Carter Falls."

"I'll have to clear it first, you know that." Rachel picked at her salad. "HE wanted to see you before you went north."

"Then HE will have to come to me." Claire ordered another eel and more tea. "I want to go home."

The girls finished their lunch and drove back to the safe house in silence. Both knew that the tall man was not someone to disregard, but Claire had made up her mind, and it looked as though this part of her personality was going to stick. Tomorrow they were going to Carter Falls.

In the morning the two women had their bags packed and were ready to leave. Claire picked up the small transmitter on the bar that she could use to contact the surveillance vehicle and spoke into it.

"Frick, please bring the car around." And then she stuck it in her purse.

When the girls exited the elevator with bags in tow the two agency men were waiting. Each, with a look of confusion, dutifully packed the bags in the back of the SUV and waited.

"Frick," Claire started. "we're going to the Carter Falls house. If you lose us, don't panic. Not much on the road can catch the Porsche. If we run into any problems we'll call you on the transmitter." Then she did something totally unexpected. She gave each a peck on the cheek. "Be dears and try not to scare the natives up there. They don't take much to out of towners, and for Gods sake don't mention you're from Massachusetts."

With a quick swirl the women where in the car and out of the lot, leaving the two agents standing in front of their SUV.

"What the hell was that all about?" Rachel looked at Claire in astonishment.

"What ever do y'all mean?" Claire did her best southern belle imitation.

"Kissing Frick and Frack. Have you lost your mind? Oh no, wait, you don't have one, that's it, right?"

"Oh relax." Claire merged onto I 293 North and hit the gas. "From time to time I like to have some fun too, ya know. I can't be Claire Daniels, dull, boring, serious, secret agent, all the time."

Rachel saw the conversation was going nowhere so she changed subjects.

"Tell me about Carter Falls. There isn't much in the files." Rachel settled in for a long drive.

"There wouldn't be," started Claire, "the town doesn't lend itself to visitors. "

Claire shut off the radio, eased into the I-93 traffic north, and began a description that she had never really thought of. To her Carter Falls was home, not where she was born and raised, but where she always went back to. She worked there as a kid during the summers, and skied in the winters. Her and Claire's parents owned the house and everybody was treated as equal owners.

"Okay, here goes. The Carters first settled in the area in the 1600s. Whether out of fear of religious repression or a wish for seclusion they brought their families from all over the English countryside to New Hampshire. The area is a beautiful mountainous landscape that had, and still has, rich soil and cool summers. The winters suck. The drifts can get up to twenty feet in sections and the temperature to one hundred below zero with the wind chill. Did you know that New Hampshire holds the continental United States record for cold at 47 below on the top of Mount Washington with a two hundred mile an hour wind?"

Rachel shook her head no.

"Anyway," Claire turned onto 104 and sped back up. "game was plentiful, the crops flourished, the fish were fat, and logging prospered. Somewhere in the 1700s the religious nature of the area changed. What had been a Puritan based settlement took a darker turn and reports of witchcraft and sorcery abounded for the next hundred years. Those from the cities that ventured too deep into the Falls, as the natives called it, never came back. By 1850 the Carter family controlled all the industry in the area and if you were not a Carter, you basically were not welcomed. A quick turn onto Highway 25 put her closer to their destination. At that time Ezekial Carter began to recall all his books and manuscripts that he had loaned out to museums on the subject of black magic and the family went into an even deeper seclusion. He also began buying everything he could on supportive subjects and stacked them in the mansion on the top of Sweat Hill. Writers like Bearse, Poe, and Lovecraft, whose aunts had a house in the Falls, and were Carters, would come to visit and research. The Carter collection of H. P. Lovecraft is the largest in the world, twice the size of the special collection at Brown University."

Claire turned onto Route 16 and kept going.

"How did your parents become residents if the town is so closed?" Rachel looked out at the spring scenery. It was austere in its simplicity, the trees, fields, a few farms, and small towns.

"The house was left to all four of our parents by my great great grand mother. Even before my folks were out of grammar school in Manchester, they jointly owned the house and land. I think that's what cemented their engagements: the house. My mother said once that the will stipulated that if she and her brother, did not marry the other sibling pair by the time they were twenty two, the house was to be burned to the ground and the soil salted. Now what the hell that meant I never figured out, but after high school my mom and dad and Danny's mom and dad got married."

Rachel caught the reference to Danny but said nothing.

"Claire was the expert on the Falls." Claire continued. "She did her Ph.D. thesis on the Falls two years ago."

"I never knew your cousin had a Ph.D.." Rachel sat up as the Porsche began to slow into a small town.

"There's a lot the agency doesn't know." Claire pulled into a small Texaco station and stopped the car. Reaching into her purse she pulled out the transmitter.

"Frick this is Claire. We're at the Texaco in the Falls. We'll wait for you here."

She put the radio back in her purse and smiled. "I may be reckless at times, but I'm not stupid. This is not a friendly place, even if you do belong here. Let's get a drink and I'll finish your history lesson."

Five minutes later, back in the car, Claire with her trademark Moxie, and Rachel with a Diet Coke, Claire started talking again.

"Some time ago, I don't know exactly when, the Carters decided to donate their collection to Brown University. At that time they had already moved the entire collection to the tunnels under the library, over there." Claire pointed to an old, brick and wooden building up an adjoining street. "This town is crisscrossed with tunnels, for when you couldn't get out in the winter. Some of the larger ones were renovated with temperature and humidity controls and now houses the Carter special collection. The Carters also donated enough money to build a digitization center to put all the works on digital discs. After that Brown gets everything."

An old woman walked up to the car from the driver's side and stopped. Rachel bristled and reached for her pistol, but held off showing her hand.

"You the Daniels girl, ain't ya?" The woman looked Claire in the eyes.

"Ayuh." Claire looked back at the old woman and smiled. "Ain't seen you for some time. How you been?"

"Been slow." The woman replied. "Ain't hit bottom yet, but when I do I guess I'll know." She leaned over the car a little closer. "I was real sorry to hear bout your cousin. Nice boy. Used to steal apples as a kid from my backfield. I used to let him. He was real good to the land. Never even broke a twig on the tree."

Claire suddenly realized that this woman was Hannah Carter, the librarian's sister. Miss Carter as the town called her was one of the oldest residence in the Falls. When Danny used to sneak into her fields for apples, he thought she was ancient. That was thirty years ago. How old was she?

The old lady began to move off. "You come over to the house some time soon. I'll tell you things about your parents you didn't know." And then she was gone.

"Jesus." Rachel relaxed and slid the Glock back in its holster. "That was bizarre."

"Nah," Claire stared off as the lady walked out of sight, "that's the way the Falls are."

The black SUV pulled up behind the Porsche and stopped.

"Hit the head and get a drink. We'll leave when you're ready." Claire shouted out the window.

When everyone was back in their respective vehicles the two car convoy started off. Claire's house was only three miles up the road. Rounding the last turn she drove up a gravel driveway and parked the car under a large woodshed roof. The SUV parked in front of the house and the agents got out.

The farmhouse was rambling, to say the least. Over the last two centuries at least three additions had been added to where the house looked like an architectural nightmare. There were dormers, and gambrels everywhere. A widow's walk was on the south side of the third floor, looking out over the pastures. Lead glass intermixed with storm windows, which in some places had been replaced with thermopane. There were four chimneys, and what looked like a vent for a forced hot air furnace.

Rachel followed Claire through the mudroom, off the shed to the kitchen. There was a smell of fresh bread in the air, and something was cooking in a large crock-pot. The heater had been turned up to sixty-five and a fire was burning in the main living room. Rachel expected a butler to step out of the shadows and ask for their coats.

"The house is clear." Frack called from the top of the second floor landing.

"Ma'am," Frick walked into the kitchen, "I don't like this. The front door was unlocked and the house has been visited recently."

Claire walked over to the center counter and picked up the loaf of bread wrapped in a towel. Underneath was a small note that said

'Welcome Back'. She put the loaf down and lifted the cover of the crock-pot. There was a stew cooking, probably deer from the smell, with new potatoes and baby carrots. The base smelled like wild garlic and chives.

In the double fridge Rachel found fresh fruits, vegetables, condiments, milk, two six packs of Moxie, two of Diet Coke, a bottle of Rachel's favorite wine, and beer. Claire, Rachel, Frick and Frack stood in the kitchen amazed.

"Someone has gone to a lot of trouble to make us feel at home." Claire heard the timer on the coffee pot go on. The hot, black liquid started pouring into the glass container.

Frack walked over to the pot. Smelling the fumes he turned to the girls.

"It's chicory. I used to drink it when I was still married. I loved the taste."

"Now this is getting really weird." Rachel sat at the counter. "Who knew we were coming here and who had a key."

"The locks don't work." Claire cut a piece of bread and dipped it in the stew. "We have internal security when we're home, other than that we just leave the door closed. There isn't much here to steal and Carters don't usually travel far from their front doors."

At that everyone else started eating. The bread was wheat and the meat was indeed deer, with pieces of what Claire said was rabbit. After lunch the bags were unloaded and unpacked. Frick and Frack took rooms on the second floor. There were seven bedrooms in the old house, one for the housekeeper on the main floor, four on the second floor, where Frick, Frack, Mac and Myers would sleep, and two on the top floor. Rachel and Claire took the two top rooms: one being hers from before, and one being her cousins.

"I feel funny taking your old room." Rachel called across the hall.

"Danny wouldn't have minded." Claire yelled back. "You're the best looking girl that ever slept in that bed."

Rachel walked into Claire's room and sat on the bed.

"That's the second time today you've referred to Danny in the past tense." Rachel started folding underwear that was piled in a heap on the bed. "Do we need to discuss this further?"

"You know it's strange." Claire grabbed the pile of underwear and stuck them in a drawer. "I know I'm Danny but I look at my life and Danny is so far away. I wonder when this is over who I'll be." She picked up her bras and put them next to the underwear. "And then I'll say something as Claire, and I *am* Claire, not just filling her clothes or her shoes, but *her*.

Rachel gave the red head a strange look.

"Not Twilight Zone stuff, but more an intuitiveness." Claire finished packing and sat next to Rachel. "It scares me sometimes. Claire and I were so different. She was hard and sometimes cruel. Nothing got in her way, I guess because she was a girl, and had to work harder. Old lady Carter was right about the apples and me. I would bring a snipper with me so as not to damage the tree. Claire would go hunting with the men every fall and winter. But now I'm supposed to be Claire, do I become hard like her?"

There were no answers. Both women knew they were in uncharted waters. They spent the rest of the day checking the house, testing the security, preparing for the summer. At dusk Frick found Claire out in the back storage shed sitting on a hay bale.

"You alright Ma'am?" He stood next to her and looked around.

"Burns," Claire had never used his real name before, "do you have a family?

"No ma'am. Never had time. The agency was my life."

"Yea, mine too," Claire got up and the two of them started walking back to the main house, "and my death."

34

CHAPTER THREE

0730 hours, May 10, 2001
Just Nails Salon
Mall of New Hampshire

Denise Ng unlocked the door of the salon and walked into the dimly lit back room. The door to the front portion was ajar and she could barely see the outlines of the tables and chairs in the room. Odd, she thought, that the alarm was not on. One of the other girls must have come in and then gone out for an errand. It was something that they did, once the store was opened the first time. It saved time.

Walking rather quickly through the shadows; she could probably have walked through the store with her eyes closed, she reached the light switch. Flicking the switch up the lights came on. It was then she saw her booth mate lying on the floor, blood spreading out from a single hole in her back. Denise tried to scream but something closed around her mouth. Struggling, she was slammed against the wall. A single, quiet, automatic round ended the struggle.

The assailant dropped the girl where she was. Reaching into his pocket he pulled out a small pocketknife and neatly cut her right index finger off. Putting it in a plastic baggie, already holding another one, he stuffed the baggie in his pocket and walked out the back door. In another fifteen minutes the owner would come in and find the mess. Let him do the clean up.

0900 hours, May 10, 2001
Carter Falls house

When Rachel and Claire came into the kitchen for breakfast, Mack and Myer were already eating. Frick and Frack were in the sitting

35

room, the formal reception area just off the dining room, where they were setting up the briefing and computer equipment. Mack and Myer didn't look anything like their TV counterparts. The original comedians had been older and always wore wild outfits as they went from one adventure to another. This team of Mack and Myer were both very young, very buffed, to use Rachel's terminology, and had a lot of teeth; something Claire found disquieting.

Myer, whose real name was Hogan, gave a wide, Texas smile, and greeted both ladies.

"Y'all gave us quite a scare yesterday." He continued eating his fruit loops and chocolate skim milk. "The tall dude was livid when he found out y'all came up here early."

Agent Dunbar, alias agent Mack, brushed his hair out of his eyes, adjusted his glasses and finished his coffee.

"You could have at least warned Burns and Dougherty." Mack put the cup in the sink. "Poor bastards didn't even have a toothbrush last night."

At that the two agents began laughing uncontrollably. Obviously it was funny, at least to them.

Losing the grin Myers looked at Claire, "He says to be here at eleven for a compressed video conference." and walked out the room.

"Pay no attention to Hogan." Mack walked past the girls. "He didn't get any sleep last night because of this. Poor baby had to pack the van. Usually sleeps most of the shift."

Claire looked sheepishly at Rachel and grinned. "Seemed like a good idea at the time."

The girls laughed for a few minutes then had breakfast.

At exactly eleven o'clock the video screen filled with the face of the tall man. The six chairs in the make shift conference room in up state New Hampshire were filled. Claire and Rachel had the couch, Mack and Myer sat at the table, and Frick and Frack took straight back chairs from the dining room.

"What the hell did you think you were doing yesterday?" The tall man was always straight to the point. "Do you know how much has gone into this operation? You could have been killed."

Claire knew that taking the blame would have been useless. The choices had been made. Rachel, sitting next to her friend, knew that if she had not gone with Claire, Claire would have gone alone. Frick and Frack did what they were told by whoever was senior at the time: nothing more or less.

"For the moment," HE continued, "we believe you're safe. There is no indication that Levesque knew where you went, although if it were I, I'd figure it out pretty quickly. Claire, you know him better than anyone else living, but in return he knows you better than anyone else does, also. It won't take him long to show up in the Falls."

"Why would he show up here?" Claire leaned forward on the couch. "He got what he wanted when he killed Danny."

The tall man ignored the question and continued.

"I'm preparing a full report of everything we have up to date. I'll send it up by courier as soon as I finish it. For now, stay alive, and for Christ sake stay out of the spotlight." The screen went black.

"Well," Rachel said, getting up, "that went pretty well."

"Did you notice how he ignored my question?" Claire sat on the couch for a moment and thought. "It was as if he expected Steve to pack up and head north."

"You know." Rachel walked to the window. "He always seems to know where Steve is going." The black girl watched birds fly north across the muddy fields. "When I was first called, it was as if he already had the plan in his mind."

Rachel motioned Claire to follow her and the two women walked out onto the front porch, leaving the male agents to their work.

"I was jogging when the attack happened at the Embassy." Rachel sat on the steps, her long wool skirt catching dead leaves and grass from the wind. "I arrived as they were wheeling you out of surgery. HE told me that you were going on undercover assignment and that I was to be your partner, but also to watch your reactions to how the situation progressed."

Claire sat down next to Rachel and stared across the fields. There was a prickling feeling in her neck, so she pulled up her collar.

"HE had me review medical texts of gender dysphasia and mental

37

conditioning while you were in recovery." Rachel continued. "HE kept sending me journals on how hormones slow reaction time, how fast skin recovers after surgery, what the largest implant is possible with no pre-structured skin conditioning. Really weird stuff."

Rachel stood up and walked into the yard. Turning back to the house she said.

"I can't prove anything, but I'd swear that he knew exactly what was going to happen from the time you were shot until now."

"Follow me." Claire walked around the back of the house and toward the barn. "HE never called me Danny from the first day in the hospital. I was always agent Daniels to him. When I left the hospital I was taken to Claire's apartment, not my loft."

"I remember that." Rachel broke in. "HE had me meet you there. Within a week I was living there."

"I never understood that either." Claire opened the barn doors and walked in. "Why so much security. If Danny was the target, why care if I was alive?"

"Are we back to Danny and you again?" Rachel asked.

"Don't start." Claire shot Rachel THAT look, that only women can do.

"Anyway, it just never figured." Claire began pulling off another mitten from a car in the middle of the barn floor. "What do you know about HIM?"

Rachel sat on a hay bale and watched the redhead work. "I never met him before that night at the hospital. I asked around the agency about him and no one even knows his name. They all call him the tall man."

Claire took the cover off the 1962 MGA. She opened the driver's side and sat down. The top was off the car, and from the rust and dust Rachel didn't think it had run for years. Claire just kept talking.

"Do you know I've never been back to my loft?" Claire played with the steering wheel. "I tried to go back once, but the keys didn't work. By that time no one would have recognized me anyway, but I was careful not to talk to anyone I had known. The family across the hall that had moved in after I was shot said the tenant had been killed, and that the loft was for rent. It was kind of funny, really, I spent all that time there and when it was over I had nothing to show for it but some boxes in storage."

"Yea, but you also got a great pair of breasts out of the deal." Rachel ducked as the piece of floor matting sailed above her head. Claire was grabbing another piece when Rachel ran behind the car.

"I told you, this is not forever." Claire sighed and went back to fingering the steering wheel.

The quiet man hidden in the grasses at the other end of the field had been there for two hours before the girls walked out onto the porch. He had followed the black SUV from Manchester when Mack and Myers brought the equipment. Working his way around the fields was easy, since he knew each and every tree and rock in the valley. He and Danny had spent their youth growing up around here every summer when Steve's parents would let him vacation with the cousins.

Now he was watching the house with a pair of binoculars when Jackson and Daniels exited. Steve had not seen Claire since the night at the Embassy. He couldn't believe she survived. He saw the round go right through her. Every time he got into a position to approach her the agency or that black bitch would get in the way.

After the girls walked around the back of the house, Steve waited for another thirty minutes before crawling away. Safely out of sight he stood up and walked back to his truck. He had rented a cabin up the mountain and the drive was only a few minutes, however, it gave him a view of the road just south of the Daniels farm, so he could tell when and which way the vehicles were going.

It started raining that night and continued for four days. Claire and Rachel spent the time researching the town and it's surroundings by reading the original Claire's notes and dissertation. In the beginning of one of her notebooks they found a bundle of old letters and papers. By themselves, even though they were odd, they weren't sufficient to cause alarm, but together they gave Rachel an uneasy feeling about the entire area. Claire, on the other hand, just wrote it off to the Falls, and kept reading. The cover sheet was the one that really set the stage for the cold, rainy day:

They say that only humans can be evil, that only humans have the capacity to know right from wrong, but I think that *they* are incorrect. I believe that other things can be evil as well. I believe that animals can be evil, that tools and carriages and houses can be evil, and I believe that entire towns can be evil.

Carter Falls New Hampshire is such a town. It is old and dirty and dark and evil. Edgar Allen Poe vacationed there. H. P. Lovecraft had a summer home there that his aunt left him. Ambrose Bearse was there the month before he disappeared. Coleridge never visited there. If he had his fiction may have been more brutal, more vicious, and he would probably have gone mad like some of the current residents.

I know of this town because I lived there, loved there, and escaped from there. I would still be there if my sense of self preservation had not compelled me to run on a cold snowy night to my horse and ride until I saw the lights of civilization far to the south. This is a warning to anyone who may visit there. Do not stay long or you may stay forever.

The most important find, however, in the notes was a detailed diagram of the tunnels below the main town. Where the library had expanded to form the archives, there was more detail inked in, and some of the tunnels were just penciled dotted lines, but Rachel figured there were over fifty miles of tunnels scattered all over the area. What was of particular interest was one tunnel that seemed to run from town to the Daniels farmhouse.

Finally the sun shone on the fifth day and everyone started feeling more positive. The four support agents, with Claire's help, built a file on Steve and all the dealings that he had been involved with. Rachel worked on a psychological profile of him, and Claire filled in that also from them growing up together. It was late that afternoon that boredom got the best of the women.

"I want seafood." It was a statement, flat and out there. "Rachel, get dressed, we're going to Conway."

Before any of the male agents in the house could say anything, Claire added. "Which team is going with us?"

Mack and Myer were up immediately. "We'll go."

"Then be ready by six." Rachel raced Claire to the top floor shower.

At five thirty when Rachel walked into Claire's room she couldn't believe what she saw. Claire had chosen a skintight pair of Lady Wranglers. Somehow she had tucked everything out of sight and got the pants to fit. The legs were tucked into black cowgirl boots with three-inch heels. She had found a black knit long sleeve pullover that showed every inch of her. Almost to add insult to injury she had chosen not to wear a bra, even though the doctors had said to support her implants for at least two weeks, and the large nipples cast shadows on the material. Thankfully she had passed on the black Stetson that Rachel saw in the closet.

"Are we going for sea food or to a rodeo?" Rachel laughed until she fell on the bed.

"I'm trying to find what I don't like in the closet. I figure I'll wear everything and throw out what doesn't work for me." Claire spun around in front of the full-length mirror.

"And *this* works for you?" Rachel got off the bed and left the room.

"Well," Claire said demurely, "it does make a statement."

Rachel in her customary wool skirt and jacket preceded the cowgirl from hell down the stairs. At the landing Mack and Myers were waiting. Myers gave a whistle when Claire stepped off the stairs.

"Damned if you don't make me homesick for Austin." He caught himself too late. "I mean," he stuttered. "that's a fine outfit you're wearing agent Daniels."

Claire smiled at the two men as Rachel whispered in her eye. "Yea, it makes a statement."

The back roads of up state New Hampshire are not what you would call friendly. Logging trucks and snow plows take their toll on the asphalt, and at points it looks like a snake was followed up the hill and then paved. Switchbacks and deep curves were rampant.

In the winter the really bad roads were closed to all but local traffic but in the spring and summer most were at least drivable. The trip through Freedom and Madison and into Conway took about forty minutes. The trip was uneventful and the girls talked about the scenery and food. Mack and Myer had never seen trees and brush so thick. Myer was from Texas and Mack was from New Jersey, where if you saw a tree, it was probably dying. The cars pulled into a small strip mall on Rt. 16, next to the Fryeburg bank building, and stopped.

When Yankees think of lobster they usually think of Barnacle Billy's in Ogunquit Maine. Years ago the owner of Billy's opened a small fish market and lobster house in Conway to service the tourist trade. From the first day it had been a great success and was usually crowded. Tonight was no exception and the four agents had to share a table in one corner of the small room.

In the middle of their meal a dirty hand slammed itself onto the wooden table and tipped over the butter dish.

"Well bitch. Remember me?"

The four looked up at the ugliest face they had ever seen. The boy was about twenty-five with a flat nose, acne scars, grease on one ear, and brown teeth. His tee shirt was yellow with sweat stains and his pants smelled of motor oil.

Everyone at the table was ready to shoot the kid but Claire seemed to be in control of the situation. Rachel noticed that her entire demeanor changed.

"Someone as ugly as you would be hard to forget, but I must have been successful." She continued cutting her lobster tail with a steak knife.

"You broke my nose with a beer bottle." The kid was playing for effect.

"Didn't seem to do any harm to your looks." Claire dipped a piece of lobster in the melted butter, put it in her mouth with her knife and savored the flavor.

Seeing that the woman in front of him was not going to break down the roughneck tried a different ploy. "I'm going to enjoy having

42

those pretty tits of yours." He grinned.

Everything seemed to happen at once. Claire spun the steak knife and drove it into the table between two of the kids fingers. She grabbed his belt, and pulling his pants opened, dumped a glass of ice water down his crotch. Looking up with steel blue eyes she said. "You can have my tits when I'm done with them. In fact I'll shove them up your ass for you."

With all the commotion the waitress appeared and asked if everything was okay. The kid pushed his way out the door and disappeared, and Claire, back to being cute, asked for another glass of ice water. "You never know who else might visit." She said.

After supper they left the restaurant and knew something was wrong. The SUV was sitting on two slashed tires next to the Porsche. Scanning the parking lot Rachel saw the kid sitting in an old Ford F150 with two others. Getting the doors to the Porsche open, Rachel jumped in. Claire reached into the car and pulled two levers. Suddenly to the black girls surprise the roof came off in one piece, and quickly Claire had it stored in the trunk. Getting behind the wheel she just had time to close the door before the Ford came within a hairs breath of ripping it off the hinges.

"That bastard." Screamed Claire. "Nobody hurts my car."

The two males, guns drawn, were standing next to the car, waiting. The Ford had stopped at the other end of the parking lot, about seventy yards away, and waited.

"Guys, this is between them and me. No one talks about this later, okay?" The two men nodded. "Get the tires fixed and meet me back at the farm. I'm going to take hayseed and his friends on a tour of the country side."

Without another word the Porsche was out of the lot and onto Rt. 16. She had to slow the car down so the truck could catch up to her before she hit Highway 153.

"Reach into the glove box and grab that canvas bag." She shouted to Rachel over the noise of the wind.

Rachel found a small green canvas bag at the bottom of the glove box and pulled it out. It felt funny to the touch.

"Be careful with those." Said Claire, "They're sharp as hell."

"What are they?" Rachel looked into the bag but could only see what looked like nails.

"They're called tetsu-bishi. The ninja used them to stop pursuers because they always land point up. They'd play hell with the soft zori sandals. The French called them caltrops when they were made larger for the Maginon Line during World War II. A tank would drive over one and couldn't help but show its belly. These are pointed and made out of tungsten steel. Tires don't stand a chance."

The car took a couple of sharp curves and the headlights of the truck following were lost in the shadows. Turning left at a sign that said Snowville Lodge Claire slowed a little and gave the truck time to catch them.

"Now I have fun." Claire had a strange smile.

"Get ready to throw those over the back of the car. But be careful not to hit the car." Rachel thought that the car was more important than their health. "Make sure you get them in our lane I want all four tires out on the truck."

Ripping down a straight section of road for about a mile, Claire called, "Get ready." The car traveled another two hundred yards. "Ready." The headlights showed a sharp curve ahead when Claire yelled. "Now."

The caltrops sailed out over the back of the Porsche and scattered across the roadway. Immediately Claire shut off the car lights and pulled over and backed into an enclosed road, hidden from view.

The greasy kid, thinking that the car was far ahead sped up to catch the red headed women. He could think of nothing but beating her to death. None of the passengers in the Ford saw the caltrops on the road. By the time they heard all four tires erupt, they were in a slide off the road and down a shallow embankment into Snowville Pond. The greasy kid driving was driven into the steering wheel, and had the wind knocked out of him. The fat guy by the passenger window struck his head into the windshield and snapped back into the seat. The kid in the middle was crushed by his friends but sustained no injuries. By the time Claire drove the Porsche out of the brush and headed down the road, back to the farm, the kids were dragging themselves up the embankment toward the main road.

They sat on the roadway until a car stopped just short of the sharp nails in the road. A single man walked up to the three and shone a light on them.

"Not a good night for a swim, huh?" They couldn't see his face, but figured he must be a state cop by the way he held his light high in his right hand.

Shining his light out onto the truck in the lake he said. "Look's like your truck is sinking."

All three kids turned sharply to look at the truck that hadn't moved an inch since it struck the water. Three rounds, three more bodies. Steve tossed the severed fingers into the woods across the road. Some animal would eat them before they were found. 'Nobody gets to her before I do' he thought to himself and drove away.

Claire and Rachel reached the farmhouse about a half hour later. The ride back had been less harrowing. Even though Rachel was a trained field agent, her specialty was psychology. Road chases and fights in restaurants were not things she did everyday.

Claire on the other hand acted like it was a regular day in the park. She cruised back through the countryside listening to some golden oldies station.

Mack and Myer were waiting for the girls when they pulled up. Even though she had called to say she was safe, they still feared for their charges like overprotective mother hens to two lost chicks.

Frick and Frack had gone to Laconia for groceries and pulled in right behind the Porsche. After an explanation of what happened, and an understanding that no one mentioned any of it to the tall man, they called it a night.

"Hey Claire." Rachel walked into Claire's room. "Who were you tonight?"

Claire got a far away look for a moment and then said. "I think I was Claire." She put on an oversized flannel pajama top that came to her knees, and rolled up the sleeves.

"I think that kid was the one that Claire broke his nose last year.

She told me some guy grabbed her from behind at a bar in North Conway. She said she hit him with the first thing handy, which was a longneck bottle. When she left the bar he was crying in the corner with blood pouring out his nose." She began brushing her hair.

"But who were you when you almost cut the kids hand off?" Rachel pushed the question.

"Oh, I was Danny then." Claire kept brushing. "Claire would have spiked his hand to the table with the knife. "But," Claire put down the brush, "when he tried to hurt the Porsche I just lost it. I thought, *that son of a bitch*, I spent years working on this car and nobody is going to screw with it. It was my car, not Claire's or Danny's but mine. Does that make sense?"

"No," laughed Rachel, "but nothing else does either."

Steve beat the Porsche home by a few minutes. He took his regular position in the brush and watched until all the lights went out. Staying in the shadows he worked his way around to the back of the house and into the barn. Checking every inch for surveillance devices he methodically went from building to building looking at each exterior. Secure that nothing had been installed outside he walked away from the farm. He knew what kind of security system the house had inside. He and Danny had installed it years ago. What no one else knew, however, was that he had programmed an override to the system that only he knew. When the time came, the house was his.

CHAPTER FOUR

May 14, 2001
Daniels farmhouse

Claire was up late that night. While everyone else slept, she paced the house, checking the windows and doors. There was more to this than she could see. She looked at the situation as Danny would, emotionally, trying to justify what was happening. Finding no answers there she looked at the situation from Claire's viewpoint. Growing up Danny had always envied Claire in the way she could compartmentalize a situation and then solve the problem. She never seemed bothered by the motions that drove circumstances. There were just the facts.

Sitting in the rocking chair in her bedroom she began thinking the situation from the beginning. They had been shot. Claire had died. The tall man and Rachel showed up. The tall man said that Danny had been the target and that he, Danny, would have to become Claire for safety and security reasons. No excuses had been accepted. Become Claire or join Claire. Treatment had started the third day after the incident.

Six months of intense training to become Claire Daniels. Danny had never been given the chance to remember who he had been. Everything had been Claire: Claire's memories, Claire's clothes, and even Claire's friends. A week before the implants Rachel and Claire had gone out with some of Claire's friends from the agency. Using silicone falsies to give the impression of fuller breasts, the night went off without a hitch. Four of Claire's oldest friends couldn't tell the difference.

But why? Think girl, Claire thought. What is missing? They had been after Steve for months. Why that night? She opened the bay windows and walked out onto the widow's walk. Danny had asked his father once why it was called a widow's walk. His father said the sailor's wives would have them on the top of their houses where they could watch for the sails of their husband's ships. Danny never understood how anyone could think you could see the ocean from Carter Falls.

The air was still cold in the valley and she huddled deeper into her robe. What if Danny hadn't been the target? Was that it? What if Claire was? That didn't make any sense either. If Claire was the target, then why the elaborate hoax to create another Claire, unless she was the decoy? What if the tall man couldn't get to Steve any other way but have him try to kill Claire again? For the first time in her life her stomach turned.

Switching her attention to another question Claire closed the doors and turned on the light at her dressing table. Looking at the map of the tunnels she tried to estimate how far the one ran toward the farm. Had Claire found the entrance during her research?

Around three she got into bed and went to sleep. She knew less then than she did at midnight, but she was going to find out.

Steve Levesque also paced at his house. He couldn't believe he had missed killing Claire. The round passed straight through her. There was no way she could have lived, yet, he saw Claire. He knew her better than anyone alive. They had grown up together, dated, had sex, had fallen apart, and become best friends. Claire Daniels was alive; at least for the time being. Why did the agency send her here to the Falls? Didn't they know that she was an easy target here? Steve knew every inch of the Falls. He had hunted it for years with Danny. Why put Claire in harms way?

Then it hit him. The agency thought the target had been Danny. Danny died in the barrage. The first three rounds had struck Danny across the chest. Steve had never learned how to control a machine pistol with his left hand. He could fire an automatic or revolver with his left, but the force of a machine weapon needed too much control. If he still had his right trigger finger it would have all worked out, but that small item had paid for a lot of things earlier on.

They must have sent Claire on vacation after the shooting. They could be working on an entirely different assignment by now, she and that black bitch shadow, and those four suits that never paid attention to anything. Over the past six months Steve had walked past each of them at least a dozen times without the slightest degree of recognition. He'd wait for his time. He wasn't foolish enough to think that he could just walk up to Claire say hello and kill her, but for now, he had time to plan.

May 15, 2001
Daniels farmhouse

In the morning Claire, dressed in jeans and a sweatshirt, her hair tied in a ponytail, came down early. She had jumped on Rachel's bed a few minutes before eight to alert the girl that they were going for an Uncle Wiggly. Back when Danny and Claire were kids there was a game called Uncle Wiggly. Whenever their folks would get lost on one of their digs they told the kids they were on an Uncle Wiggly, meaning they were lost, but moving forward in a brisk manner. The idea stuck with the kids as they grew up and whenever they needed to just get away, they would head off on an Uncle Wiggly.

Rachel was similarly dress, ready for the dirt and dust of the tunnels below the city. It was Claire's intention to find the tunnel that headed back to the farmhouse. If she could find it, so could Steve.

Taking Frick and Frack with her the four of them went in the SUV. Burns and Dougherty camped out in the reading room of the town library as the two women headed down the narrow stairs to the basement. Each had a copy of the map that the original Claire had drawn. The two women made an interesting pair as they walked through the library. Both dressed in jeans, Rachel had her Glock in a waistband while Claire wore hers under her left arm. A web belt held water, ammunition, a flashlight, a radio, and a small portable respirator.

"May I help you ladies? Oh, it's you." A very old lady came out

49

from the back of the room as the girls reached the bottom of the stairs. Claire remembered her as Hester Carter, the head librarian. It was Hester's sister Hannah that had first greeted Claire when they stopped at Ralph's Texaco.

Claire, putting on an act for the old woman walked over to her and laid the map on one of the old maple tables.

"Miss Carter," Claire said slowly, "I apologize for this but I can't remember some of the things I've done in the last year. I remember this map, but can't get it oriented to the directions anymore. Could you help me?"

The ancient librarian looked down at the map and turned it 90 degrees. "This is how we're sittin' now." She looked at the young red head and smiled. "I was real sorry to hear bout your cousin Danny. Couldn't ever get him in here, but he was still a good boy growing up. Real shame to die like some cinema movie character."

Miss Carter reached into her bun of hair for a pencil. Taking her glasses off her chest, where they hung by a gold chain, she put them on and started drawing on Claire's copy of the map.

"I led you astray with this map." She dotted lines with her pencil. "This tunnel caved in in 81. This one," she erased some lines and dotted others, "follows the natural caves under the town till it ends here." She put her pencil back in her hair.

Claire, looking at the map and realized that Miss Carter had drawn the dotted lines not the original Claire. "Did I ever ask you if one of the tunnels leads up to my farmhouse." She asked.

"I always 'spected you to but you never did." Miss Carter turned to face the southern most door in the small room. "That door there leads to a fork. The left fork, here on the map," she pointed to a spot on the map with her finger, "leads to an incline that I'm told goes toward your place, and maybe beyond. Ain't never been in the tunnels myself, much too dangerous for these old bones." She went to her desk and sat down.

"Ma'am, "Rachel interrupted, "how do you know about the tunnels then?"

The old lady gave a toothy grin. "I'm a librarian. It's my job."

As Claire and Rachel walked through the back door into the basement portion that led to the tunnels Miss Carter called after them. "You come by some times soon." Looking at Claire. "Me and Hannah will tell you things about your folks you don't yet know."

"Jesus," Rachel whispered as they entered the first tunnel, "is everyone weird around here?"

"I'm starting to think you may have something on that." Claire took the lead. "The map says there's a fork up ahead."

At the first fork they took a left. The map showed another fork ahead, and they took a left at that one also. They had been walking for about two minutes when they found another fork.

"There's nothing about this fork on the map. This tunnel should go straight for another two inches." Rachel looked at her map.

"Is that two map inches, or two real inches?" Claire giggled.

"Map inches, silly." Rachel poked the other girl in the ribs. "This isn't like men: real inches or imaginary inches."

At that Claire started to laugh heavily. "Seven months ago I wouldn't have even understood that." Claire wiped a tear from her eye. "Now I won't get that image out of my head all day. Thanks."

Looking down at the dust on the tunnel floor Rachel said. "There hasn't been anyone down here for years. You go right. I'll go left. Walk for five minutes. If you don't find anything indicating which tunnel is which, meet back here."

"Sounds good to me." Claire struck off down the tunnel. "See you in ten."

A couple of minutes later Claire saw a light ahead and off to the right. Knowing that there should be no one in the tunnels she switched off her flashlight and pulled her pistol. Rounding the corner she saw an old man in overalls and work boots, sitting on a rickety straight back chair against the tunnel wall. Next to him and causing the light was an old kerosene lantern on the ground. Claire walked closer to the man and stopped.

"You can put that gun away, son. Ain't no need fer protection down here." The old man looked at the girl with a benign smile on his face.

"Do you know me?" Claire holstered the Glock.

"Sure I do." The old man returned. "You're Danny St. Claire, from up the hill. Ain't seen ya in, what, twenty-five years." The old man scratched his head. "Yea, bout that."

Claire was too shocked to think about asking how he knew she was Danny. She just stood there and stared.

"You got a lot to learn son. Get up to Hannah's house soon as you can. She's a batty old bird, but her memory is the best in town. Can't have you and that friend of yours running round half cocked." He started to chuckle. "Get it, half cocked?"

"Claire, you up there?" Claire heard Rachel call from out of the darkness.

"I remember you." Claire turned back to the old man. "You're old man Carter. I used to mow your yard during summers as a kid."

The old man nodded. "Did a right fine job of it too." He said.

"But I saw your funeral. I watched them bury you. You're dead."

"Course I am son. But so are you."

"Claire, you there?"

Claire turned back to look at Rachel coming into the light of the lantern.

"Where'd you get the lantern?" Rachel stopped and took a drink of water from her canteen.

"Mr. Carter had it." Claire turned back to the chair but it was empty.

"Who?"

"Old man Carter was sitting there when I came up the tunnel." Rachel looked at Claire cautiously. "Really. He was sitting there and we talked. He said I needed to go see Hannah, and he called me Danny." She hesitated to tell her friend the rest.

Rachel walked over to the chair and picked up the lantern. "We're the only foot prints." She held the lantern high in the air to look around. "Look's like we've been the only ones here for some time."

Claire gave a shrug and could say nothing. She knew what she saw and heard. "Did you find anything at your end?" Claire asked.

"Nothing as exciting as you." Rachel started forward down the tunnel, holding the lantern ahead of her. At least Claire had found a light she thought. "The tunnel I followed ended about two hundred yards past the fork. There was a ladder leading up to a trap door, but I didn't try it. I came back to find you and heard you talking."

"So you did hear the old man?" Claire felt vindicated.

"No, just you. When I came around the corner there you were standing in front of the chair with the light on the ground."

In another thirty minutes the girls came to the end of the tunnel. There was a great wooden door on forged iron hinges blocking their way. The oak was as strong as it had been when it was put up, which by the look of the nails, was at least seventy-five years ago. There was a large key lock on the hasp. Rachel pulled at it but it wouldn't budge. They would have to come back with tools to get past the door.

Unable to go forward, they opted to go back to the ladder that Rachel found and see if that led anywhere. Retracing their steps, and with the lantern's light, they found the fork and the ladder. Carefully Rachel climbed two steps until she could touch the wooden trap door. Pushing on it gently it moved upward. Not certain where she was she pushed the door a little more until she could see into the upper room.

From her vantage point she could see a rug on the floor, and furniture legs. There was sunlight coming in from somewhere and she thought she smelled bread. A little more and she could tell the door led to a parlor or sitting room somewhere.

Suddenly a pair of shoes appeared from her left and she lost her grip on the wooden door. It slammed down on her head and she stumbled to the tunnel floor. As she stood and shook off the dust Claire climbed the ladder and opened the trap door about a foot. There were the shoes still in front of her. They were attached to a pair of legs in heavy gray stockings.

"It's about time you two got here." A women's voice said. "Come on up out of that damp tunnel. You'll catch your death of cold."

Claire pushed the trap door fully open. She and Rachel climbed out of the tunnel into the living room of Miss Hannah Carter, matriarch of Carter Falls. Claire closed the trap door and adjusted the throw rug. By the look of the hard wood floor, the rug covered the entire opening, when not in use, which seemed like most of the time.

"Would you girls like to clean up before we have cookies?" Miss Carter acted as if their visit was the most normal thing in the world. "Daryl said he saw you down in the tunnels, but didn't tell me you were going to stop by. I just now baked a new batch of Toll House for your visit."

The old lady walked back to the kitchen and the girls stood there for a few seconds.

"Bathroom is at the end of the hall." Came the voice from the other room. "Towels are above the sink."

Once in the bathroom with the door closed Rachel grabbed Claire by the arm.

"Now this is out of control." She was visibly shaken. "Was Daryl who you saw in the tunnels?"

"I think that was his name." Claire ran the hot water. "Hell I was twelve when he died. How can I remember what his name was?"

Rachel washed her hands and face and the two of them just stood there.

"Are you sure he's dead?" Rachel calmed a little.

"Oh yea, I'm sure." Claire said. "I even said to him 'you're dead'. Do you know what he said to me then, just before you came around the corner? So are you."

Hannah laid a tray of chocolate chip cookies and three glasses of cold milk on the coffee table. When the girls reentered the living room she motioned them to sit on the couch and she sat across from them in a big stuffed chair.

"You two have had quite a time since you got here." Hannah took a cookie. "And you dear," looking at Claire, "such an ordeal the last six months. It's a wonder you look as good as you do. Before you go I'll give you something for the scarring. Grandpa used to use it on us kids when we'd cut ourselves in the fields. Anyway, I'm glad you visited. I wanted to talk to you about your folks."

Claire was about to say something but Hannah put up her hand. "I know what you're going to say, which folks? Am I right?" Claire nodded. "Does it matter? All four of them pretty much count as one in the Falls."

Claire was completely confused. She and Rachel sat there and listened without saying a word.

"Your folks were Carters. You probably didn't know that because your mother and father didn't want the stigma of the Falls to fall on you when they left. Your mother and uncle are Carters from my side of the family. Goes back almost two hundred years. Your father and aunt's side of the family married into the Carters about ninety years ago. Before that they were from Plymouth I think."

Rachel ate her cookie and drank some milk. Claire just sat there.

Hannah continued like some demented tour guide on a four-hour boat trip through Hell. "We needed to get your folks together so we left them the old farmhouse. Never did like it much. Always had a draft. Even in the dead of summer there's a breeze. Daryl said it was from the way it sat on the hill. He should know, it was he who remodeled it before your folks got it."

Hannah drank some milk and took a deep breath. "Anyway, your folks got married and then they moved. Tried to tell them they needed to stay and continue the work here in town but they were teachers and they just up and left. It wasn't until after you were out of school that they started coming back. Spent a lot of time in the tunnels, they did. Most of what we know about them come from your dad. Right smart he was about old languages and cultures."

The old lady continued looking straight at Claire.

"After they died we thought that was the end of it. The rest of us are too old to continue the research. Hester will get the books on computer and off to Brown before she dies, but the tunnels may have to be sealed. Can't have some flatlander wandering around down there and getting lost. That's why we were so excited when Claire did her research on the tunnels for her Ph.D.. It's your job to finish the project that your folks started."

"What project?" Claire asked, quite agitated. "And how did my parents die?"

"The farmhouse will tell you the first part and you'll figure out the second when its' time."

The two women moved a little as if to leave when Hannah again put up her hand and they immediately sat back on the couch. It was as if a giant hand had pulled each against the soft cushions. Looking at Rachel Miss Carter smiled.

"You look so much like your great great great grandmother. She was a Carter also."

"I beg your pardon?" The comment took Rachel by surprise.

"Elyse was her name." Hannah offered the black girl another cookie. "Her grandmother had been a slave just before the war. A young man from Effingham, just across the river, bought her in Memphis. He was about twenty and she couldn't have been more than fifteen. Brought her back to New Hampshire, freed her and married her. He was a Charboneau.

They had a son named Robert. He was a good-looking boy with deep dark brooding eyes. He married a Carter girl from up past Sweat Hill. They had three girls, the middle one being Elyse. She married some no account businessman from Portland and they moved south. I knew eventually someone from your family would come back here, but I never thought it would be with Claire.

"Oh my heavens." Cried Miss Carter. "Look at the time. You poor girls must be starving for dinner. I'll have Jacob take you back to the farm. He's waiting out by the garage with the truck."

"Thank you but we have people waiting on us at the library." Said Rachel.

"You mean those nice boys with the black truck. Hester sent them home as soon as you went into the tunnels. No telling how long you were going to be there. Your friends had nothing really to do and with their guns and all, like to frighten some of the town folk to death. Anyway, Jacob will drop you off and Claire, tell Sheriff Rogers that the dill is ready to plant outside now."

The old lady got up and helped the girls out the front door. Although it had been before noon when they came up through the trap door, it was dark and the clock tower over the church showed nine-thirty. As promised a man of about thirty was waiting by a blue Chevy pickup. He was wearing overalls and rubber boots, but he was clean and smiled when the women approached.

"Evenin' Claire." He bowed his head a little. "Evenin' to you Miss Jackson."

The three of them got in the cab of the truck and he drove up the hill to the farm without another word. Once in front of the house the girls got out of the truck and he drove away.

"Boy, not one for conversation." Rachel looked over at the Grafton County Sheriff cruiser by the side porch. "Looks like we have company."

"My money is on Sheriff Rogers." Claire walked up the stairs.

"No way." Rachel came up after her. "Your town is too strange already."

"Not my town anymore." Chided Claire. "It's your town now, also."

Sheriff John Rogers was about sixty-five. Gray hair and too heavy to be anything but a small county law officer he moved with a gait that only comes with practice. He'd known the Daniels and St. Claire kids all their lives. He had once tried to date Stella Daniels, Claire's mother, when they were all in high school, but to no avail. Instead, being an athlete and good-looking, he had chased and captured the heart of the prom queen. Forty-eight years later they were still together with five children and seventeen grandkids around the county.

The five men in the room all stood when the ladies entered. Mack and Myer were in shirtsleeves and slacks. Frick and Frack were in jeans and tee shirts and the sheriff was in his uniform.

"Evening Claire." Said the sheriff. "It's been a long time."

"Uncle John." Claire gave the big man a hug. "It has been a long time.

Rachel looked at Claire strangely.

"John was always around to get us out of trouble when we were kids. It was easier to adopt him than avoid him." Claire told the group. "What do we owe the pleasure? I know it's not for my cooking." Claire had been a notoriously bad cook all her life.

"We found three local boys dead on the Snowville Road, their truck was in Snowville Pond." The sheriff sat back down where he had been previous to the girl's arrival.

Before Claire or Rachel could respond Myer cut them off. "Seems they were shot on the bank of the Pond."

Claire stopped what she was going to say and walked over to the fireplace. Rachel had gone to the kitchen for a Diet Coke, and she brought back a Moxie for Claire. Taking a sip, Claire started telling what she knew.

"John, they tried to kill us." She put the can on the mantle. The bright orange of the can was a stark contrast to the aged red cherry wood. "Last year one of them grabbed me at a bar. He wouldn't let go so I hit him with a beer bottle. I thought that was the end of it. Last night he showed up at Billy's. Basically he threatened my life, and when we left the restaurant our SUV tires had been slashed. He and two others chased us down 153 until I took the Snowville turn."

John was taking it all in. Rachel expected the big man to fall asleep; he just sat there and nodded from time to time.

Continuing, Claire said. "I knew the pond was high so I threw out some tire shredders to send them into the water. I figured that would cool their tempers enough to think about what they were trying to do. You know me John, if I have to kill someone I will without a moment's hesitation, but these were just stupid kids. Anyway when we drove away they were climbing out of the water. We came straight back here and went to bed. Pretty much end of story."

Everyone in the room waiting for what the sheriff was going to say next. The story was pretty cut and dry from the agent's points of view.

"I've followed your career, and Danny's too, for as long back as I can remember. I know who you work for and I believe you when you said you left them alive, but there is something else that struck us as very odd."

The sheriff shifted his bulk in the chair. "All three of them were shot in the back, one round each, and their right index fingers were severed. We looked for the fingers at the crime scene but couldn't find any trace." Rogers pulled a slip of paper from his pocket and looked at it. "You were shot in the back weren't you?" It was a rhetorical question. Everyone already knew the answer.

"Yes." Claire leaned against the fireplace. "But I have all my fingers." She held up her hands, fingers spread.

"Sheriff." Rachel broke in. "What kind of weapon was used?"

"You know that's strange too. Ballistics is having a hell of a time matching the rounds. We pulled two good ones out of the bodies, but they don't match anything American. We sent them to Concord for further study. Should know in a couple days." The sheriff got up and headed for the door.

"When I heard you were back here I hoped it would be quiet for you, especially after the past six months. I wonder if some people can find peace and quiet, or if activity just seems to follow them from one situation to another." He put on his hat and walked out onto the porch.

"John." Claire called after him. "I almost forgot. Miss Carter says you can put the dill out now."

"Good," he returned, "looks like it will be an early plantin'. Full moon is this Friday. Stay away from the graveyard. You're too young to start." With that he was in his car and out the yard.

Spinning around Claire started giving orders.

"I want a full data dump on the three dead at the pond. Frick, get into every database you can and find out what really happened. Frack, I want to know if this is the only killing like this. Mack, I want to know everything the original Claire did the last six months before she died and Myer I want a bio on Steve since he left the agency. You have till morning. Rachel," she softened her tone, "let's make hot chocolate. Anyone else want some?"

Once in the kitchen the two girls started comparing notes.

"I was thinking last night about this whole mess." Claire put a pot of water on the stove. "What if, and this is only one option, Danny was never the target? What if I, I mean Claire, had been?"

Rachel got the chocolate mix from the cupboard and started

reaching for cups.

"I thought that also, but why? Why kill Claire now?"

"Something happened just before the shooting. Something that Claire or Danny did that pushed Steve over the edge. He operated for fifteen years without worrying about the agency, why now?"

Rachel grabbed a tray with cups and spoons and Claire took the tray with the hot chocolate and they re-entered the work area.

"Don't get used to this but here's your hot chocolate." They put down the trays.

"No cookies?" Mack took one of the cups. "My mother always tucked me in with cookies."

Claire stepped on his foot lightly with her hiking boots as she passed by. "Your mother doesn't work here and I don't tuck anyone in." Everyone started laughing at that and the tension of the night was broken.

On her way up the stairs to bed Claire gave one more order. "Someone find out who the hell the tall man is and how he's connected to all this."

At the top of the third floor landing Rachel was sitting. As Claire climbed the final steps Rachel got up and waited.

"Are you too tired for girl talk?" Rachel asked.

"Bath first." Said Claire.

"You take the top one, I'll use the one on the second floor." Rachel came out of her room with towel and soaps. "The boys will be another couple hours tonight by the looks of it." She headed back down the stairs.

By midnight the two women were sitting on Rachel's double bed. Claire had opened the bottle of wine in the fridge and brought up two glasses. It was a little too sweet for her taste but Rachel had said it was her favorite.

"Okay kid," Claire offered a toast with her glass, "you called this meeting."

Rachel clicked her glass and sat back against the headboard.

"I need some answers." She sipped her wine. "First, how did your parent die? And I mean all of them. If Miss Carter is going to treat all four of your folks as one unit, who are we to argue? Second, What is so special about being a Carter? Until two months ago I had never even heard of this place, now it's supposed to be my Brigadoon? Three, What's so important about the tunnels? Finally, why are you and your cousin so damned important to this town?

"Boy you don't want much, do you?" Claire emptied her glass and poured another. "Okay first things first. Claire and I were away on assignments when our folks died. They were somewhere here in town doing work on one of the old mills. They were archaeologists at Dartmouth, but had taken a year sabbatical to research the history of the town. As you saw today the tunnels go everywhere, and one of them collapsed, crushing all four of them. They were buried before we got home. When we asked the funeral parlor where the graves were no one would tell us. I think it was Win Carter, the guy who owned the funeral home that said some things are better left alone. Nothing we did or said would budge any of these people. After five days up here in this house, beating our heads against every wall in town we went back to Washington. That was eleven years ago. I haven't been back here more than ten times since then. Claire used to come back every chance she got. She thought that the more she learned about the town; maybe she could find their graves. Toward the end the deeper in the history of the town she got, the more insistent she was that something other than a cave in had happened to our folks. We never had time to talk about it before the shooting."

"I need to pee." Rachel got up and went to the bathroom down the hall. Returning quickly she poured another glass of wine and said. "One down, three to go."

"As far as I know," Claire continued, "there is nothing special about being a Carter. It's like being a Charboneau in Effingham or a Brooks in Freedom, or a Chick in Madison. Every town has its local family that has spent generations farming the area. The Carters have just been more secluded. Never having been a Carter, at least not knowing it, I never gave it much thought. Danny and I wondered why our folks were given this house, but when no one gives you answers you eventually stop asking.

61

As for the tunnels, as a kid we thought they were just neat. We would try to get into them every chance we had, but we were always kept out. As we now know they run for miles, and if Hester is correct there are caves to add to the tunnels. We need to get past that wooden door, I think, to get some of your answers. Before snow plows the tunnels around town were the only way to get from house to house. A lot of the schools and villages have the same kind of tunnel system that dates from the 1700s."

"That leaves the big question of the night." Rachel poured half of the wine still in the bottle into Claire's glass and drank the rest from the bottle. "Why are you and Danny so important to this town?"

"Don't you mean me and Claire?" Claire emptied her glass and held it between her fingers.

"No I mean you and Danny." Didn't you say the guy in the tunnels said Danny was dead?"

"Yes," replied Claire, "but he said he was dead too, and I talked to him."

"That means nothing in this place." Rachel looked at the bottle in her hand. "It's like this bottle. It's not empty, even though you don't see anything, you just can't see what's in it."

"That is too deep for me tonight. I'm going to bed. See you in the morning." Claire staggered slightly to the door. The wine was stronger than she had thought, or she was just not used to drinking anymore.

"Claire?" Rachel asked. "Who are you?" She expected some smart-ass answer like she usually got. Instead her friend looked tired and said.

"I'm a Carter."

CHAPTER FIVE

May 16, 2001
Daniels farmhouse

Claire dreamed all night. She was on a beach digging and making sand castles. Danny was with her, helping, and their parents were down the beach. Every time she would get something carved out of the sand, or made a tunnel through a castle wall the waves would pound on the ground and the sand would fall in on itself. At one point there were other people on the beach helping her dig, but the same thing always happened. She kept calling for Danny but he was digging in one spot with a small steel shovel. He was throwing the sand all over the place with each scoop. Screaming at one point she looked up to see him holding a big rusty iron key. A giant wave crashed down on everyone on the beach, washing away Danny, the key, and all the sand and she woke up.

She lay there for a few minutes and then drifted back to sleep. Again the same dream. She woke four times that night, experiencing the beach scene five times. In the morning when she looked in the mirror her eyes were bloodshot and her skin was pale and wan.

Rachel tossed and turned all night. She dreamed that she was in a great cave. There were black and white people all around her, but she didn't know any of them. Whenever she would touch one they would dissolve into smoke. In the middle of the cave was a fire burning. Black African women and men danced around it while a fat black woman cut the head off a chicken and spread it's blood around the circle. The language was foreign to her, but she recognized it at the same time. The drummers beat a strange rhythm, louder and louder until the girl awoke in a sheet of sweat.

On the way back from getting a glass of water in the bathroom she heard Claire thrash in bed. Rachel crawled back into hers and fell asleep. Instantly she was on an island with palm trees and sea breezes. The hills were covered with lush vegetation and the natives; the same from her first dream, were dancing around a great fire. Drums and chickens were everywhere. As the great knife fell on one of chicken's neck the blood spurt across her naked breasts and into her hair. Someone called to her but instead of Rachel she was called Ntambi. She took the limp chicken and shook it at the crowd dancing around her. Screaming something she threw the dead bird into the fire and woke up.

She got out of bed and looking into her mirror saw an old black woman with white hair and two teeth missing. Rachel looked behind her quickly and saw nothing. When she again looked into the mirror she saw herself, long straight hair in disarray, her eyes bloodshot and sunken, her skin with a sickly pallor. 'God I look like shit.' she thought.

Rachel walked into the bathroom to shower as Claire was walking out. Each looked at the other and at the same time said.

"You look like Hell."

Two hours later each girl looked better. With clean clothes, makeup and strong coffee for Rachel, and tea for Claire they settled into the situation room, as they called it and started working. The weather was turning nasty, with chances of strong thundershowers all day so they decided to stay home and work.

The four male agents had a pile of papers in front of them. Each had worked most of the night on their respective assignments, only getting to sleep a few hours ago. It was noon when Claire was ready to be briefed. She seemed to take charge without moving. One moment everyone was talking and working and the next minute they all turned to her as one. Realizing that the attention was on her she began with Frack.

Pointing to the short, balding man, wearing two days of facial hair and a crumpled shirt, she said. "Frack, what do you have?"

"This is only a draft, you understand." Frack always started this way, and then usually had volumes to say. "Counting the three dead kids at the pond there have been fourteen similar deaths in the last six months."

The number was shocking to Claire. How could so many similar murders have taken place and she didn't know.

"Does that include the dead guy we found in the Lexus?" Asked Frick.

"Check." Said Frack.

"What dead guy in the Lexus?" Claire shouted.

"Back in Manchester, the morning you took the Porsche to the Mall Burns found a dead street person in the Lexus. We cleaned it up just before you got up." Frack said.

"Why the hell didn't anyone tell me about it?" Claire was livid.

"To be honest you were being a shit and besides we reported it to base. They replaced the Lexus with another one and sent the whole car to Boston." Frack waited for the fallout to settle.

Claire realized that there were personnel issues that needed to be settled. Lowering her voice she tried to console the five others in the room.

"Look. We're all in deep shit. Someone or some group has targeted me, and possibly you since we're all here together. No more secrets, no more attitudes, and that also includes me, okay?"

Everyone nodded in agreement and Claire went on. "Now please agent Dougherty, keep going."

Frack, not used to being called by name, sat there for a moment until Frick elbowed him. Realizing that the red head was talking to him he started again.

"All fourteen deaths were killed by the same person. The method was a single Czech round to the back, with death almost always instantaneously. After that a sharp knife cut off the right index finger of the victim. No trace of any finger has been found. The first victim was a gas station attendant at a Shell station in Washington on October 1st. The next worked at a clothing store a week later. Three more in Nashua, a doctor and two nurses, a father, mother and one daughter back in Washington at Danny's old apartment building, in fact the family across the hall from his, two nail girls at the Mall of New

Hampshire and the three kids in the pond. Add the one in the Lexus and it comes to fourteen."

Everyone looked at Claire. She sat there with a shocked look on her face, the color completely drained from her. Finally composing herself she whispered. "The Shell station was where I got gas the first day out. Rachel drove but it was down the street from Claire's apartment and the kid wouldn't shut up about how beautiful Rachel was. Was the clothing store a Liberty Station?" Frack nodded. Claire continued. "That was the girl who helped me buy new skirts. I needed something comfortable that fit the bandages from the shooting. I talked to the family at Danny's loft when I tried to get back into the apartment. They lived across the hall, with a three-year-old girl. A three year old! You can figure out the rest." Claire took a deep breath. "Everyone I talk to or come in contact with is being killed."

Rachel stirred in her chair and asked. "Why not me?" I've been with you from the start?"

"Probably because you two are never out of sight of one of us or each other." Mack came back.

"These people that were killed were killed in out of the way places or at night. The killer is not exposing himself yet for the main kill." Frack gave in analysis.

Claire looked at Frick. "Next."

Frick picked up a piece of paper and put it back down on the table. "What the sheriff told us last night is pretty much what is on the wire. The ballistics hasn't been matched yet, but my bet it's the same Czech pistol. Probably a CZ 52 automatic pistol, 7.62 x 25 mm; standard issue to most Czech secret police departments and intelligence agencies. If Steve is the shooter, and I think it is safe to assume that, then he probably picked up the weapon after Baghdad."

Claire nodded and turned to Myer. "Next."

Myer began his history on Steve Levesque. "Steve was assigned to lead a team to extract an Iraqi business leader who had ties to Hussein. When the team got to Baghdad they were shot up pretty bad in an ambush. The contact and most of the team got out. Steve and three others were reported killed. One agent said he saw Steve hit with rifle fire and go down. They tried to get to him but were cut off by Iraqi Special Forces troops. Radio Baghdad that night reported four American spies were killed while trying to assassinate Hussein. Nothing more reported on him until three years ago when he was linked to an Embassy bombing in Caracas. Since then we have linked him to over a hundred deaths. Some say he works out of Prague, where the government gives him protection, others say Belfast where he works for the Irish Republic Army. If he's using a CZ-52 then he may be closer to Prague. I'll have a contact in Prague ask around as soon as I get done today."

"Good." Claire swept her bangs out of her eyes. She needed her hair trimmed. "Do that."

"Finally we get to Mack." Claire smiled at the Texan. "Okay cowboy, y'all up."

Mack smiled at the cute red head, caught himself when he remembered it was a man behind those deep blue eyes and started talking as fast as he could.

"Danny St. Claire did nothing out of the ordinary for eight months prior to the shooting. He worked five days a week, spent his weekends working on an old car at a storage facility in Alexandria, and then had Sunday night dinner with his cousin Claire Daniels. Danny never left the country, or even the Washington area the entire time.

Claire Daniels kept basically the same schedule. She worked five days a week and on Friday night would drive to Carter Falls until Sunday afternoon, when she would return to Washington and have dinner with Danny. She left the country once, two weeks before the shooting to go to Berlin.

"Why?" Asked Rachel this time.

The trip report said she was to investigate a double agent that was selling both sides short. According to the report she tracked down the agent at a bakery in East Berlin. For some reason, probably efficiency, she shot the agent once in the back and left the country. The leak has been reported sealed. Nothing else pertinent to the situation."

Claire began to make a connection to some things, but still had a ways to go to connect all the dots. She finally asked.

"Who had the tall man?"

"I did." Mack said. "Real name Jason Allen Avery. Worked for the CIA until a car bomb took out his hearing in one ear. After that his equilibrium was screwed so the Agency traded him to the NSA. He became a free for all problem solver. My sources say that before Danny was wheeled into the emergency room at Bethesda, Avery was on his way from Washington to oversee the operation. He called for Rachel by name on his cell phone from the hospital. Told the assignments officer that he wouldn't have anyone but her. Nothing else was available on such short notice."

"Assessments people at two o'clock. Let's get lunch and then" She was interrupted by the ringing of the telephone.

Rachel reached over to the end table and picked up the cordless. "Hello. Who may I say is calling? Just a minute." Putting her hand over the receiver she turned to Claire. "Do you know a Michael Bishop?"

Claire looked at the four males in the room and made a motion with her hand toward the computers. Immediately Mack started a trace on the call. Frick had the identification database start searching for Michael Bishop and Myer started the recorder. Taking the receiver from Rachel she answered the call.

"This is Claire. Michael so good to hear your voice again." She shrugged at Rachel and continued. "Where are you calling from?"

"He's in Laconia." Said Myer to Frick. "Check the Laconia area."

"I'd forgotten. That's so kind of you to say that. I don't know if I can. I haven't been able to since my accident. You didn't hear? I was shot last year at work. No nothing serious just in one side and out the other. Yes it can ruin your day." Frick interrupted her.

"Got him." He whispered.

"Michael can you hold for a moment my soup is boiling. No I won't put you on hold, just be a dear and give me a second. You can continue talking if you like."

Claire looked at the note that Mack handed her.

Michael Bishop owns a bar and Karaoke club in Laconia. Seems to be a friend of Claire's. 60ish, married, two kids.

"That's better. Can't let the soup boil over. I have friends from work up for the month on vacation." Claire made a yack yack motion with her hand. "Okay if you insist but don't expect much. Okay. Love you too. Bye."

"Great," Claire handed the phone back to Rachel. "He expects me to sing at his place in Laconia on Friday. He says be there at eight sharp and wear my green dress with the sequins and do Reba. Do I have a green dress with sequins? And who the hell is Reba."

Claire had never been laughed at so hard in her life. Everyone in the room burst out at the same time and Rachel almost fell to the floor.

"Honey," Rachel gasped, "have you ever heard of Reba McIntyre?" She wiped tears from both eyes and stood up.

"Oh Christ," Claire moaned, "you mean I have to sing country?"

"I'm sure y'all will be right fine, Miss Daniels." Myer gave it his most deep Texas drawl. "Ah only wish I could be there to wish you well."

"Shine up your buckle, cowboy, we're all going Friday night. If I make a fool of myself, I want a fast getaway." Claire clapped her hands. "Now let's have lunch. As I was saying before the interruption, assessments at two."

Claire grabbed Rachel's arm as they walked through the dining room. "Do I have any Reba tapes?"

"You have a stack on your dresser, next to the CD player." Rachel gave Claire the 'what planet have you been on' look. "And I would bet that the garment bag in your closet is the green dress."

"How do I get into these messes?" Asked Claire

"Just lucky I guess." Was the answer from Mack as he passed them in the front hall.

At two o'clock the group was again assembled in the conference room.

"Assessments?" Asked Claire.

"I went out with an Allen Avery last year." Rachel said and everyone looked her way. "He was a real loser, but he kept asking me out so I went out of pity. There were about eight of us that night, so it wasn't like a date or anything, but he thought we were meant for each other. Kept calling me all summer. Finally in August I told him if he called or wrote me again I would have to report him."

"What was he like, was he tall?" Claire questioned.

"No he was real short and dumpy. Had all the spy gadgets and drove a vette. Thought he was James Bond with the ladies. He gave me the creeps."

"Run a check on Avery." Claire ordered. "It may be a blind lead, but let's run it. Anything else?"

"If you shot some woman in the back there may be a connection to the killings and the shooting at the Embassy." Offered Frick.

"I did not shoot anyone in the back." Claire corrected. "That was the other Claire, I mean, cousin Claire. Oh hell, forget it." Claire shook her head and swept her hair away from her face with her left hand. "Check it out anyway, may be something. Also check to see if this girl has any connection with the Czechs."

"I hate to say it," broke in Mac, "but it looks like all leads point to you at the moment."

"I have to agree with him." Said Rachel.

"Me too." Added Frick.

"Alright then let's assume I am still the target and Danny was a casualty of war." Claire made a mental note to stop putting himself in Claire's position. "What do we do now? Brief me at nine tonight on what you find. I'm going to listen to country music and then barf."

"We sure do got faith in you Miss Reba." Called Frack from behind the computers.

Grabbing a Moxie from the fridge Claire trudged up the stairs to her room. Reba she thought, great. Once there she found the stack of CDs on the dresser next to the player. There was even one that said Laconia on it. She put it in and lay on the bed. As the first chords of 'Why Haven't I Heard From You' came on Rachel jumped on the end of the bed and the can of Moxie shot all over Claire's shirt.

"Gonna git some country?" She giggled.

70

"You think this is funny, don't you?" The red head wiped Moxie from her face and hands. "This is some kind of demented torture that you approve of."

"Relax." Rachel tossed a towel to her friend. "You need a break. Someone is trying to kill you. You just learned that the world you knew really sucks and tomorrow may not be a better day. Everyone needs a little lightness from time to time." Rachel reached over and took the stack of CDs from the dresser. Thumbing through them she asked. "How many of these are you going to do?"

"As many as I can." Claire started listening to the music and reading the words on the jacket insert. "If this is my penalty for being Claire, then I may as well be the best Claire I can for that night. I just wish I could sing."

"You can't sing?" Rachel was stunned. She assumed that since Danny and Claire were so similar they both could sing. She had heard that Claire sang like a rock star.

"Never really tried." Claire said. "I sing in the bath and in the truck, but on stage? God this is going to be a" And she left it at that.

Going to the closet Rachel pulled out a black garment back that said Prada. Inside was a floor length, green sequin dress that was cut down the front to the navel, down the back to the spine, and up one side to the knee. She wondered what kept it on. Holding it up to Claire she gave a grin.

"Here is your wardrobe for Friday."

Claire looked up, groaned, and buried her face in her pillow. Hanging the dress bag back in the closet the black girl left the third floor to sounds of 'The Heart is a Lonely Hunter'. It would be Friday night she lamented.

Around five Claire descended to the world of the working. She had had enough of country music for now and longed for some blues. When she was Danny she had always listened to singers like Billy Holiday and such. What happened to really good blues? Everyone else was in the conference room typing or writing. They all stopped when she entered but she motioned for them to continue. After a moment she cleared her thought.

"Has anyone seen a pile of sand or a sand box around the farm?" The question could not have been more bizarre. The four men just stared at her as if she had lost her mind.

"No really, this is not a trick question." She repeated. "Has anyone seen any sand piles or areas of sand anywhere around the property?"

No one spoke for a few minutes and then Frick said. "There's a sand bar at the turn of the river," pointing to the back of the house, "down the bank behind the barn. I saw it the first time here when we dropped your stuff off. Glen and I ran a sweep of the area to get fields of fire."

Claire thanked them and went away. As she passed through the back door and into the back yard and the light rain, Rachel caught up to her.

"You going to build sand castles to relieve stress?" She asked.

"No, I'm going to look for castles in the sand to answer questions."

"You lost me on that one." The two walked past the barn and into the brush behind.

"I had a dream last night." Claire pushed her way through the bushes. Climbing down the hill to the water Claire told Rachel the dream. Rachel in turn told Claire hers and they both realized why they looked like hell this morning. "No more wine before bed." Claire said just before catching her foot on a root and falling the last three feet to the water. Landing face first she jumped up and screamed.

"God damn that water's cold." She was standing in about two feet of freshly melted snow running at about five miles an hour.

"I can tell." Rachel commented. "Your nipples have never been harder."

With chattering teeth Claire retorted. "Again with the nipples. Did your mother breast-feed you as a child? You have this tit fetish."

"Not all tits," returned Rachel, "just yours."

"After this is over they can put these in you." Claire walked over to the sand bar. "You'd look wonderful with your own dinner shelf." She looked around the bank, oblivious to her wet clothes and the cold weather. When I was growing up this brook ran about six feet higher. This sand bar was never here. "This is it." She grabbed a stick in the sand.

The stick turned out to be a short metal shovel used to clean out fireplaces. Claire got down on her hands and knees and started digging in the sand.

"What are you doing?" Rachel waded across the brook to the other side. The water was freezing. She couldn't understand why her friend wasn't blue with frostbite.

"Gotta keep digging." Claire shouted over the steady rain and the water. As soon as she would have a hole dug the water would seep in and cave in the sides.

"Claire, there's nothing there but sand." Rachel grabbed Claire's shoulder.

"No it's here." Claire shook of the hand. "I just have to dig faster." She picked up the pace and started flailing at the sand. Careless as to where the sand went, Rachel was hit more than once with a shovel full.

"Stop it!" Rachel shouted.

"Is everything all right?" Mack and Myer were standing at the top of the hill looking down into the gully.

"Claire, stop digging." Rachel again tried to grab at the shovel.

Slipping on a wet rock the black girl fell on one knee and two hands. As she rose to both knees she heard something metallic and saw a dark object fly past her and into the water. Claire was on it instantly. Casting the shovel aside she reached for the object with both hands and cried out.

"I knew it. I knew it had to be here." In her hand was a great iron key, slightly rusted, and with a single iron ring attached to the end.

Rachel and Claire helped each other up and they crossed the water to the bank. Mack and Myer reached through the underbrush and pulled the two women up to the top of the hill. Claire, not letting go of the ring, let the two men lead her and Rachel back to the warmth of the farmhouse.

The sunsets quickly in the mountains, especially when it's raining. By the time the four of them reached the light of the back porch it was almost too dark to see. Claire and Rachel went upstairs to get dry clothes and Mac and Myer went to their rooms to dry off.

Claire stripped naked in the middle of her room and stood with the key in her hands. She held it like a prized possession, which considering the circumstances was a fair statement. When Rachel came across the hall in a dry skirt and sweater, Claire was still standing there, her back to the door. Rachel could see the lines of her shoulders, her waist, the full butt and powerful legs. From her angle it was hard to accept that the woman standing in front of her had been one of the best male agents in the NSA seven months ago.

"Are you okay?" Rachel walked around to Claire's front.

Claire looked up still holding the key. She was dry by now, standing over the heat vent in her room. There was a far away look in her eyes and she took deep breaths that caused her breasts to rise and fall. Three white scars, each about the size of a nickel showed on her pale skin.

"You need to get dressed." Rachel took the key from Claire and tossed it on the bed. "Here," she handled the naked woman a long sleeve flannel shirt and a pair of briefs. Once Claire had those on she walked over to her closet and grabbed a long corduroy skirt. "Your dream told you where to dig?" Rachel picked up the key and turned it over in her hand.

"No." Claire took the key from Rachel. "I just thought that sand would lead me to it."

She carried the key back downstairs and all six again took their places in the conference room. At a few minutes before nine Frick began the meeting.

"Claire," he said softly, "we've been talking about the last few days." He turned to the other men for support. "We all agree that we'll follow you two into whatever you have planned, but we need to know what else is going on."

Claire tossed the key to Frick. "Would any of you believe me if I told you that a dream last night told me that a shovel in a sand pile would lead me to the key that unlocks the great wooden door at the end of the tunnel, that runs under this entire area? Would you also believe me if I said that I think that there is a way into the tunnels from this house, or somewhere around here? Would you think I'm crazy if I said that this town holds more secrets than we have time to discover and that the problem with Steve may be the lesser of the two issues we have to resolve?"

"Until a few days ago I would have said you and Rachel were crazy for just about anything you've done this past six months. You becoming your dead cousin, who we all either knew or met at the agency. Rachel following you around like a shadow, writing everything down that you did or do. The two of you going from agent to mall rat in the blink of an eye, but now I'd believe the devil lives in those tunnels if you told me."

"Not the devil," corrected Rachel, "but maybe something far worse."

"Hey." Claire said in a loud voice. "It scared the bejesus out of us, but we found the key to the door." She changed her tone. "Let's get on with the work at hand and accept whatever method we get to solve this case." Curling up on the couch she asked. "Who's got something or do I have to sing to scare you into working harder."

At that everyone grabbed something and acted as if they were all working.

"Very funny." Claire chuckled. "Who's got something?"

"Allen Avery was an agent at the NSA until August 30th of last year." Mac hit a key on the computer and a photo of a man about thirty appeared on the screen. "The night of the 30th Avery was having dinner with some friends at his apartment when he walked into the bathroom, took his service automatic and blew his brains all over the bathroom walls. His father, the tall man, had a closed casket, and took two days off. It was the first time he had taken time off in twenty-seven years on the job. One week later Danny and Claire were shot at the Embassy."

"We believe," continued Mac, "that Rachel was assigned to this case in the hopes that she get killed in the line of duty. Somehow, we feel, the tall man holds Rachel somewhat responsible for his son's suicide."

"Is that it?" Rachel cut in. "I wouldn't go out with him so he shot himself."

"No." It was Frick that began. "You were the final failure. Allen had a string of negative reports and failed missions. The catalyst to this was Danny."

"I didn't even know this guy." Claire snapped out of her fog to become Danny again. "How did I get involved?"

"When Danny," Frick had given up long ago trying to figure out who he was talking to with Claire. As far as he was concerned Claire was here, Danny was somewhere else. "became section chief of Far East Operations, he did so over three other agents. One of them was Avery. Avery brooded over the slight until the night he killed himself. We think that the tall man ultimately blames you for his son's death, and Rachel as an accomplice."

"Let me get this straight." Claire tried to sort out the mess. "The tall man hates Danny because he beat out his son for a promotion. He also hates Rachel because she wouldn't date his son. The son dwells on this until it gets too much for him and he kills himself. Is that what you're telling me?"

"Pretty much." They all agreed in unison.

"Is that all you have for me?" Claire got up to leave.

"Well, no." Frack said.

Claire sat back down and pulled her knees up in front of her chest. She sat like this once when she was two months out of surgery, with a short skirt on, and embarrassed two colleagues who were sitting across from her. Now she always wore a skirt that was long enough to cover those parts better left covered.

"We think we have a link between Claire and Steve." Now Claire was interested.

"And?"

"You shot Mrs. Steve Levesque in the back in Berlin, two weeks before you were shot at the embassy." Frack had lost the draw for who would tell Claire the news. "The agent that was dealing from both sides had been Steve's wife for three years. I believe the pistol he uses to kill his victims is hers."

"Wow talk about motivation." Rachel added.

"Why do I suspect that there's more." Claire returned.

"Well yes." Frack was on a roll. He stood up and went to a briefing chart by the fireplace. Pulling over the first page was a complicated diagram with the tall man, his son, Claire, Danny, Steve, Steve' wife, and Rachel on it. "It looks like this." Frack took a marker and started connecting the people.

"Steve, for some reason doesn't get killed in Baghdad. He becomes an enemy agent. He meets and marries an agent from the Czech secret police. She begins selling on both sides of the fence." He looked over at the two girls on the couch to make sure they were following him. "Meanwhile, the tall man has a son that is a loser. Danny beats the guy out for the Operations Chief. He somewhat gets over it until he meets and falls for Rachel. When she threatens to report him to the agency his depression gets to him and he kills himself. The tall man blames Danny and Rachel for his sons' death." Frack stopped for a minute to catch his breath. "Now the rest is conjecture, but we think it's pretty close to the mark. The tall man gets wind that Steve is planning to kill Claire because Claire killed Steve's wife. He sends Danny with her so that Steve can kill Danny, and resolve some of the grief over his son's death, however, Danny doesn't die. Instead he survives and the tall man sees a better opportunity. He assigned Rachel to the case and orders Danny to become Claire. We believe that Steve still thinks Claire is alive and the tall man hopes that Rachel will die in the line of duty protecting Claire." Frack put down the marker. "It is therefore our consensus that all six of us are expendable as far as the agency, or at least the tall man is concerned and it's just a matter of time before we are all killed by Steve."

Frack sat back down. "Now that's it."

"Shit." Claire got up and looked at the chart.

"Oh yea." Rachel got up and walked behind the couch. Leaning over the back she said. "Unfortunately it makes perfect sense. The grief of his son's death was such a shock that HE has lost all his priorities. There's nothing he won't do to see us both dead."

"Well I for one," Stated Claire, "have no intention of becoming one of Steve's victims. Do we know where Steve is now, or can we even guess."

"This morning a senior member of the British ruling party died in his sleep. We believe that Steve had something to do with it. If that is the case, and we think we have a paper trail out of Portland Airport to Logan, and then to Heathrow, Steve is still somewhere in England. He may have taken some time off chasing you believing that you were not going to leave here any time soon." Mac leaned back in his chair.

Claire looked at the clock on the mantle. "It's Tuesday night. We stay on the airport arrivals until we think Steve is back in the country. Meanwhile I want a plan on what to do about the tall man. I hate to say it, but he's now our problem also. Stay alert, but let's take it a little slower until after Friday night. Rachel said we need some light time. I agree, but don't get sloppy. Steve could come back into the country at any time. Finally, if the tall man calls, we stall until the weekend. I don't want to tip our hand that we know what's going on, not that we really do. Do we all agree?"

With five yea votes in the room, Claire left to go to bed. Something the sheriff said about planting kept going round and round in her head, but she was too tired to care at this point. For now there was another day. Saying good night to Rachel she turned the CD player on with all the CDs she could fit and, with a pair of headphones on, went to sleep.

CHAPTER SIX

May 17, 2001
Carter Falls, New Hampshire

Wednesday morning found the farmhouse under black clouds and heavy rains. Claire and Rachel decided that to stay in would be the best option for the day and so they settled about their respective chores. Rachel spent the morning working on a plan to flush out the tall man into exposing himself to the agency. By noon she had no ideas that were worthwhile, and a splitting headache from the moisture outside. The cold and wet of the mountains at this time of year were playing hell with her sinuses. As soon as the rain let up she was going to start running again with two of the agents. However, sitting in the kitchen with a cup of tea, was her immediate plan of attack for the migraine.

Claire stayed up in her room, listening to music, singing softly, and reading the journals and notes from her cousin. At twelve-thirty she came running down the stairs with an old magazine in her hand.

"I knew I saw this somewhere." She shoved the paper under Rachel's nose. "See, it's right here."

Rachel picked up a copy of 'Unnatural Horror' magazine, dated September 1956. A short story titled 'Dragon's Teeth' was highlighted in yellow in the table of contents.

She looked at Claire and slid the issue back across the counter. "So?"

"Read it."

Rachel knew better at this point than to argue. She took her tea and the magazine and went into the living room. Propping up two big pillows she lay down on the couch and started the story.

DRAGON'S TEETH

'It was going to be a good night for planting.' Ned thought as he headed out across the field. He looked up to watch the full moon creep out from the low hanging clouds, throwing silver rays on the bare ground.

The back gate to the graveyard was ajar when Ned entered. As the eldest Carter it was his turn to sow the Dragon's Teeth.

'Dragon's Teeth,' he thought, 'what a morbid joke to play on Carter Falls.'

Ned could remember when Mr. Piler had coined the term from Jason's adventures with the Golden Fleece. Piler had been a friend of Ned's grandfather, both schoolteachers at the Carter Falls Normal School. Piler had died two years before Tatum had. Ned could now barely remember his grandfather's face as it had been before he died. He felt the wind rise as he took out the old leather bag. No one knew where the bag of teeth came from but Ned's great, great, grandmother had been the first to use them. Somehow after being used they always returned to the bag before morning. Grimly he set about his work.

He threw the teeth as one would throw grass seed a few over every grave. The moonlight cast shadows across his lined face. Ned was sixty-seven. He would not have too many more years to do this. When he was buried his son should carry on, and then his grand son, and it would continue as it had since Henrietta Carter started it in 1752.

When the bag was empty Ned walked to the open gate. Bodies were already digging their way out of the ground, slowly lumbering over to the gate. Empty eye sockets stared blankly past Ned to the field that they were to work in. Ned fought back the urge to vomit, as he did every year, when he saw his father Francis and grandfather Tatum join the ranks of molding corpses standing behind him.

When he was sure there were no more to join him he broke out into the field and headed back to the house. Fortunately the wind was high tonight and it kept the fetid smell of rotting flesh away from his nostrils.

Without being told, the bodies took up tools and seed that had been left that day in the field and began working. Ned wandered about the field until he was sure everything was being done correctly, as if he could have changed anything, and then joined his wife by the large fire out side their tool bin.

"I'll be out there soon." He said.

"I hope to be gone afore I hafta see that." She took hold of his arm.

Ned took of his hat and his thin white hair blew in the breeze. Cora, who had been with him for forty-seven years, looked out at the dead farmers.

"It ain't natural." She shuddered. "Someone musta done something powerful wicked to be cursed with such as this."

"But without this help a lot of old folks wouldn't have food for the winter." Ned released his wife's arm. "It may be the Devil's work but God is also served."

"Served, Hell!" She cried. "Served until they die to go on helping with the plantin'." She turned her back on the fields and walked into the house.

Ned could understand her attitude. Until two years ago Cora's father had been one of the planters. Then last year he just failed to come up. Ned was under the suspicion that after so many years of working in the fields the penance was served and the dead were allowed to rest. Only those families that had been born before Henrietta Carter were subject to the rites of planting.

Whatever it was the town had done it was wicked enough to condemn it forever.

Ned watched the sky begin to lighten in the east. As the first hint of morning came the bodies stopped what they were doing and turned for the graveyard. As morning rose on Carter Falls Ned sat by the dying embers looking out over three hundred acres of newly planted ground.

There weren't as many this year. An entire field was going to hay because not enough rose to plant it. The young ones were leaving the Falls sooner, now, his own sons having gone to Portland over thirty years.

Maybe next year his grandson Davie would return to the Falls; he was to graduate from college as a teacher. Ned could only hope and wait. If no one returned to help with the sowing of the teeth a lot of crops would not be planted. A lot of people would not be fed. A lot of people would die before they had to.

As Ned watched the last sightless farmer pass through the open gate he wondered if maybe his wife was right. Maybe it would be better if there was no Dragon's Teeth. He would think about that until it was time to harvest the crops; when again the teeth would be sown.

Maybe he wouldn't sow them then. Maybe he couldn't stop from doing it. Slowly he walked into the kitchen for breakfast.

"I'll be glad when this can stop." His wife poured him a cup of coffee.

"Will it ever?" Ned asked.

When Rachel finished reading she tossed the magazine on the floor. "So?" She asked.

"So." Claire picked up the issue and sat across in a lounge chair. "What if this is not fiction. What if what Uncle John was warning us about the other night is this?" She held up the magazine.

"Oh come on." Rachel rolled her eyes and frowned. "You can't be serious. Corpses of dead Carters rise up from the cemetery to plow and sow the fields every spring."

"All I said was, what if?" Claire started to walk away.

"If you're so worried about this being real then why don't you go to the cemetery Friday night and find out?" Rachel got up off the couch and followed.

"Because even here, there are some things that are best left unknown." Claire walked back upstairs.

Rachel brought a large bowl of salad and a pitcher of water up to the third floor about three. Claire was still listening to the music and reading through the journals and notes, now scattered all over the room. The girls sat on the floor, since the bed was covered with magazines, and ate.

"After we eat," Claire got the words out between mouths of lettuce,

"I want to try the green dress."

"You're really getting into this stage thing, aren't you?" Rachel poured a third glass of water. "Are you thinking of leaving the agency and going on the road?"

"Not bloody likely." Claire finished the salad. "I still can't sing."

"Let me hear you." Rachel put the bowl, pitcher, and two glasses that had already been in the room, out in the hall.

"NO!" Claire rose and went to the closet. "No one hears me until Friday night. I don't need to be told that I suck two days from show time and then still have to go on because I promised to."

The green dress proved to be less of a problem than they had thought. Evidently Claire had gone to New York and had the dress tailor-made. Rachel had expected Claire's breasts to fall out of the dress as soon as she bent over or turned, but the dress was cut in such a way that the breasts were cradled into the fabric. Even jumping up and down, which shook some of the empty CD cases onto the floor, failed to loosen anything from the dress. Finally Rachel asked a question that she had been thinking about for six months.

"What about Mr. Winky?"

Claire was dumbfounded. "Mr. Winky?"

"Yea, you know," pointing to her friend's crotch, "Mr. Winky."

"Don't worry dear." Claire patted Rachel on the head. "Mr. Winky will be out of sight and out of mind, just like always. Shit," she laughed, "Mr. Winky."

Claire was still laughing when Rachel picked up the dishes and went back down stairs. What if, Rachel thought, no, not possible, but, what if?

At seven the six house mates met in the dining room for dinner. Rachel and Frick had barbecued ribs on the back porch over a gas grill and the boys had bought potato salad and coleslaw when they were in Laconia shopping. Myer had volunteered his famous, at least to him, recipe for rib sauce, which they all agreed was pretty good, and the beer and conversation flowed freely.

"While I was in la la land did anyone have any brilliant thoughts?" Claire almost spit out a rib onto Frack.

"Mac has an idea how to get the tall man up here." Frick offered.

"Yes, but once we get him here, then what?" Mac returned. "Hold him down until he confesses what a bad boy he's been?"

"No, but I think we can rattle him enough to make him do something drastic." Rachel looked off into space for a moment, and then seemed to come back. "I have an idea."

Myer tossed his last rib onto the plate, grabbed his beer and said. "I'm listening."

"We have two weeks to a new moon." Rachel started her plan. "If we can push him over the edge about his kid in the next two weeks he may come after us at the dark of the moon."

"That's it?" Myer asked.

"Well, I didn't say it was a complete plan." Rachel defended herself.

"No, I think there may be something there." Claire broke in. "If HE thinks that we're going public with what we know he'll have to come after us before we get back to the agency. Where is he now?"

"Sidney for a joint Australian, New Zealand, United States, England terrorist summit. His office says he won't be back until next week some time." Frick had done his homework.

"Good, then we have a week." Claire was getting that 'I have a plan' look on her face. "We need to find someone who won't leak what we know to Avery. Someone above him, who we trust. I want to have a paper trail on this if it goes south. Also I don't want HIM thinking that we suspect him. Let's work a message that we have a lead that an Allen Avery may be involved in the planning of the shooting and that he died before he could have anything to do with it. I take it you all have been using blind headers to get your information?"

Everyone nodded, realizing that only a blind header could be rendered untraceable through the computer systems at the agency. It was the only way that agents could track data without fear of compromise. "Well I want you to request everything we already have on Allen Avery through regular channels. Also request a formal explanation as to why Rachel was assigned the case."

Claire stabbed at another rib. "Go through her chain of command so that everyone will know we're interested. We continue to work the channels until HE gets back in country. Then we report to HIS superiors that we have uncovered the real reason behind the assassination at the Embassy, and request a formal briefing in Washington on the Monday after the new moon."

"I still don't see how that's going to get him here?" Mac looked over at the red head.

"If Avery thinks we're going to tell the world he planned this just to kill Danny and Rachel, then HE's going to have to come up here sometimes between his arrival back at Washington and our briefing and kill all of us. I'm betting our lives that HE'll try it with a Czech CZ-52 and make it look as if Steve did it." Claire began scribbling some notes on a paper towel. "Don't go through agency channels for these." She passed the towel to Frack. "Get them by Saturday so we can test them."

Frack took the towel, scanned it once and put it in his pocket. Rising from the table he walked out of the room and to the telephone in the conference room.

"Tomorrow," Claire was on another of her rolls, "I want Rachel and someone else to go check out the place in Laconia. Look for sniper points, road accesses, and blind spots. I can't see many people being there to hear a local band and a Karaoke singer, but if there's a lot of empty space it may afford Steve an opportunity. Finally I want to know once and for all if there's any secret entrance to this farm. Tomorrow the rest of us search from the basement to the attic." Pushing her plate away she smiled briefly. "Let's get to it. We have a lot of work to do. Good night."

The weather seemed to sap the strength from everyone, and they made it an early night. Even though they were pretty certain that Steve was out of the country, the males still kept to their schedule of four-hour watches throughout the night. Claire and Frick had installed some newer monitor equipment on the doors and windows, but nothing was foolproof and if there was a secret entrance to this house, then nothing was safe either.

Rachel dreamed of drumming and water. The great fire was before a tall waterfall. Even though the mist soaked everyone the fire kept burning with a strange intensity. The black men in brightly colored robes beat their drums in rhythm to the waterfall. Rachel danced naked in the middle of the drum circle, lit by the fire. Sweat made her skin glow, and she could see herself, as though separated from the scene, sway and gyrate, her now waist length hair cutting arcs in the night.

In the morning she had to check her body for burns from the fire, and her hair to make sure she was the way she went to bed the night before. To her relief her hair was still shoulder length and there were no burns or scars from the dancing and embers. After a cold bath, then a hot shower she felt better. By nine she was sitting with the others having breakfast, dressed and ready for the drive to Laconia.

Frick had said he would accompany the black agent. He had some grocery shopping to do at the Piggly Wiggly in Laconia, and pick up a package that Frack had overnighted. By ten the SUV pulled out the drive and headed south for the day.

Claire and Frack started in the basement. Mac and Myer went to the attic. Claire was afraid that spending so much time on the third floor she could miss something so everyone started on new ground. The basement was huge. The farmhouse had once had livestock under it, probably for heat and ease of feeding. At one end had been a hay storage area, that now was just dirt. There were stalls on the north wall, with great granite blocks holding up the carrying timbers. A root cellar was attached at the south end of the house. At one time it had probably had access to the outside, but that door had been bricked up and covered over with sod.

A few times they thought they felt air but it turned out to be the drafts from the outside, coming through a crack in the foundation. The walls were as solid as the day they were laid. The floor was hard packed dirt. There was nothing stored in the entire basement to restrict the view and they could tell where the wall sat on the foundation plate, eliminating the chance of hidden passageways.

Accepting that there was no chance of a tunnel entrance through the basement they went upstairs and started looking at the conference room and library. Sometimes during the eighteenth century this section of the house and a bathroom above on the second floor had been added. No one knew if the pad was stone, dirt, or concrete, although in this climate concrete was not likely that far back.

Checking every square inch of the fireplace in the conference room they found nothing. Likewise there was no break in the wood walls, the floor or the ceiling in either room. Slightly depressed at the failure Frick and Claire walked into the dining room about four. Mac and Myer were just coming down the stairs. The look on their faces told the entire story. They hadn't found anything either.

"Nothing?" Claire asked the obvious.

"No," said Mac, "You?"

"Nothing with us either." Said Frick.

"What about the barns?" Asked Myer.

Claire shook her head. "If there's one out there, it's no different than if someone walked in from the road or the fields." She headed for the kitchen. "Can we take it that the house is secure from the outside by covert methods?"

The other three agreed. With nothing to prove otherwise they felt certain that the house was on a solid foundation.

At six Rachel and Frack returned. Their report was nothing out of the ordinary either. The bar was called Michael's and was on the outskirts of Laconia, by the lake. Rachel said that the parking lot was quite large and there was a billboard marquee by the road with Claire's name on it and One Night Only in big letters underneath. Claire took the news in stride at this point. She was convinced that this was the second biggest mistake she had ever done, the first was going to the Taiwanese Embassy.

Frack and the other men started unloading boxes and groceries. There were Fed Ex boxes from the FBI, the CIA, three private arms dealers and the Defense Intelligence Agency. After dinner the boxes were unloaded and stored. For the rest of the night the six agents worked on individual projects, preparing. They had five days at most to be ready for some kind of assault on the farmhouse. Claire prayed that her analysis of the situation was correct. Rachel wondered if Claire's analysis of the situation was accurate. The four men were pragmatic. If this didn't work, then they would improvise.

At two fifteen in the morning Special Agent Brian Hogan, better know to the group as Mac, sat in front of his console, halfway through his shift, listening to a jazz station from Chicago on headphones. Suddenly a red light lit on one of the display screens in front of him. He double checked to make sure it was not a malfunction and then pressed the button at his left. Within thirty seconds Myer was standing next to him in the dark, pistol in one hand, wearing only his boxers.

"I'd like to see you come down like this if the girls were working." Mac whispered.

"I'd come down here butt ass naked if I had to." Myer moved a little closer to the screen. "What'cha got?"

"Heat signature, two hundred yards south of the farm, in the tree line." The two agents could see a dull red glow on the overlay of the surrounding area. When they had initially moved into the farmhouse they had buried heat sensors all over the grounds. After the first rain, they were impossible to detect, however, even in the cold mist outside they could pick up a body signature as small as a squirrel.

"Could it be a deer?" Myer questioned.

"No, the computer says human." Mac punched in some keys on the keyboard and a profile came up. "Looks like female, about five foot two, one hundred pounds."

"Damned they've got these things down." Myer was impressed with the hardware. "I didn't think they could go to that level."

"I understand now that they can detect if the target is pregnant by the differential in heat." Mac went back to the pop up. "What do we do?"

"Can we get a picture?" Myer sat down next to his partner and put the pistol on the table.

"Not without lighting this place up like a Christmas Tree. We don't have a camera that can go out that far in this mist." Mac waited for the signature to move.

When Frick came down for the four o'clock shift change the blip was still there.

"What have we got?" Frick asked, taking his place at the console and switching the radio to golden oldies out of Boston.

"Heat signature of a small girl. Been there since a little after two." Mac gave Frick the situation and went to bed.

The visitor melted into the forest just before the sun came up. By the time it was light enough to get a camera on the area there was nothing there but branches and leaves.

CHAPTER SEVEN

May 19, 2001

Claire was down at eight in the morning. She said her stomach was upset from the ribs, but Rachel thought that the show that night might have something to do with it also. Quickly taking in the situation of the pre-dawn morning she kept the crew from investigating.

"We can't take the chance that she's still out there, out of range of the sensors." Claire drank her milk. "If she thinks she's invisible, then she may come closer. Any idea who she could be?"

"Could be a curious native." Frack offered.

"Are we sure Steve is in England?" Myer asked.

"As far as we know he's not arrived anywhere through customs." Rachel cut in. "We have all available agencies watching for him, but that doesn't guarantee anything. We haven't been able to catch him in seventeen years."

"Considering this new situation," Claire said, "I want two of you here tonight while we go to Laconia."

"But we'll miss the show." Whined Mac.

"I can set up a video link from the club so everyone can be in constant contact." Frick started rummaging around in a box under the table.

"That may be a good idea, anyway. If we have anything going on at either point then the others will know." Claire dropped onto the couch. "Who's staying?"

"I'll stay." It was Frick. "I want to work on some stuff here."

"Then I'll stay too." Frack added.

"Okay let's have an easy day." Claire went back to bed. "Tonight may be more than we ever expected."

"Well at least for some of us." Someone said behind her. When she turned around, everyone was looking the other way. She gave a broad smile and disappeared.

"Rachel." Mac called after the girl softly. "A few words."

"Yea." Rachel stayed in the conference room with the other agents and sat on the now well-used couch.

"How's she doing?" He thumbed toward the upstairs.

Rachel took a deep breath. "It's hard to say. One minute she's the toughest agent I've ever known, the next I think she's a frightened little girl looking for her parents at the state fair. She's been a woman for six months. In that time she's had to learn everything real women learn in forty years. That can take its toll on you."

"Is she cracking up, I guess I mean." Mac felt badly for his charge. He had not wanted this assignment when given it because he felt baby-sitting a cross dresser was not what he signed on for at the agency, but he'd taken to the girl, even if he knew she wasn't really, at least not completely. He thought of her as a sister, one that had been away for a long time, and was trying to adjust to the family again.

"No, I think she's quite sound, considering the circumstances." Rachel kicked her feet up on the couch. "Right now I think she's scared to death about tonight. She says she can't sing."

"You're shitting me." Myer almost fell out of his chair. "She looks like that," pointing toward the stairs, "and can't sing?"

"She says the real Claire got all the talent." Rachel thought about the way Myer reacted to the comment. "Won't even sing for me as a dry run. She doesn't want to be proven incompetent before she has to get on stage." Rachel stood up. "What ever happens tonight do not, and I repeat do not, laugh at her, or tell her she was bad. She's on a very thin edge right now. This could be a very crucial night for her."

After lunch, while Frick continued to play in the conference room with wires and a soldering iron, everyone else took a nap. Rachel got Claire up at three. Drawing a hot bubble bath she stuck the frazzled red head in it, and then sitting on the toilet lid Rachel talked about small stuff wanting to keep Claire's mind off what was coming.

"Frick thinks he can have cameras up and running by next weekend in the house." Rachel started rambling. "Also he says the deliveries were exactly what you asked for. He's going to test one tomorrow morning in the basement."

"What's he using for meat?" Claire lathered up her hair and rinsed it off.

"The other rack of ribs we didn't eat." Rachel poured a cup of water over Claire's hair, where she had missed some shampoo. "What are you going to do with your hair?"

"Can you curl it?" Claire asked. "I could never get the hang of a curling iron. I'm always afraid that I'll burn all my hair off."

"Yea, we'll work on it, not too much though, but the straight thing won't work with that dress." Rachel took a really good look at Claire, for the first time. Rachel had always thought of Claire as a feminine Danny. When they had met, Danny had had short, agency length hair, some stubble from the night before, and chapped skin from being outdoors a lot. Over the months the skin had cleared, and with treatments, had softened. The short hair had grown, and with extensions, looked natural at falling to her shoulders. Laser and electrolysis treatments had eliminated the beard, and the hormones had taken away most of the remaining body hair on Danny's chest, back and butt. Even without makeup the woman in the tub was quite pretty, if not beautiful. The agency had done well in her transformation and there had been good genetic stock to work from at Danny's end.

While Claire dried off Rachel asked her if she was hungry.

"I should eat something, shouldn't I?" Asked Claire. "But nothing heavy. I feel like throwing up as it is."

"Let's back track this, then." Rachel took out a note pad and started writing as Claire toweled her hair. "Its four now. You eat a salad and drink water while the curlers are in. Curlers out by five. We need to leave no later than six-thirty to get there by eight so we do your makeup at quarter of six. At six-fifteen we squeeze you into your dress." Rachel stopped and thought for a moment. "It's cold out there tonight. What are you wearing for a coat?"

"I have a couple of Givenchys in the closet. I think I'll choose which one just before I walk down stairs." Claire padded down the hall in her fuzzy bunny slippers. Rachel remembered when she bought them at the Penny's in Washington. They were on sale and were just hideous by Rachel's standards, but Claire had declared them adorable, and bought them on the spot. Now wearing them and her pink flannel nightdress, with a towel around her head, they somehow fit.

Starting to put curlers into the red hair Rachel continued the small talk, now getting a little closer to home. "Have you considered what happens if this doesn't work?"

"Every second I've been awake for the past four days." Claire said between curlers.

"And what have you decided?" Rachel kept on applying curlers, one after another.

"You mean will I sit on the stage and cry?" Claire tried to laugh, but her head was in a vice grip with the curlers.

"Well, something like that." Rachel kept curling.

"I'll deal with it when it happens." Claire was getting nervous again.

"I think you'll be just fine." Rachel finished with the curlers.

"I think you're on crack." Claire tried to lean back in the rocker, but the curlers bit into her scalp.

Rachel went downstairs while the curlers set and brought back a small dish of salad and a glass of water.

"I think I'm really getting sick of salad." Claire took a bite. "I'll be glad to get back to work and back to the gym. I feel fat."

Rachel knew it would do no good to explain to Claire there wasn't more than two pounds of excess weight on her entire body, so she kept her mouth shut.

"Tell me about the club." Claire ate more salad.

"The place is huge." Rachel regretted saying that as soon as it was out of her mouth. "Well, actually, not huge, by our standards."

"How not huge is huge?" Claire finished the salad and laid the bowl on the floor.

"Well," Rachel didn't know if she should tell her friend this or not, so she decided to go with the truth, "the place could probably hold two hundred, by the looks of the outside. It's an old J. M. Fields store, you know, like the early Wal-Marts. Lots of empty space. But like you said, who's going to come listen to a hick band and a local Karaoke singer, right?"

Claire smiled up at Rachel. She knew her friend was trying to shield her from the inevitable. In three hours she would have to face a room full of people she didn't know, but who probably knew her, and convince them that she could sing. She sent Rachel downstairs with the dishes so she could get her head together, and work out her play list.

Rachel took the opportunity to dress while Claire was thinking. She was almost as nervous as her friend. She checked on Mac and Myer. They had taken the initiative to warm up the SUV since they didn't know that the girls would be in coats. Mac was in his typical jacket and slacks, but Myer looked like a rodeo star. His boots were shined, his silver buckle sparkled, and his black Stetson was spotless. When she looked at him he just grinned.

"Chris," motioning to Myer and using his first name, "has a crush on our little Miss Claire." Mac said. "Ain't that right pardoner?"

"I do not." Myer stuttered. "I think that she deserves the dignity of the situation." He paced around the room while Mac, Frick and Frack were seated at the dining room table. "The little lady's been through a lot in the last few months. She needs our support."

"It's okay, Chris." Rachel patted him on the shoulder. "We understand."

At exactly fifteen minutes before six Rachel sat Claire, now curled and clean, but still in her nightdress, in front of the vanity and began applying makeup. Claire had been worked on by some of the best at the agency, when they were trying to cover up the problems of the mid months of transitioning, but Claire felt she had never had someone as professional as Rachel do her makeup. The black girl moved with no wasted motion. Look here, move there, the commands were short and to the point. The base, foundation, rouge, eyeliner, mascara, and finally lipstick all went on perfect the first time. They were done in twenty minutes and when Rachel stepped back she was astounded.

Looking in the mirror Claire couldn't believe it was really she. Her blue eyes were so deep they looked like paintings. The red hair was swept up off her face in a single curl, and there were small curls off both sides of her head. Claire had chosen a pair of diamond drop earrings that had come from Paris. At the time Danny had said they were far too expensive for two stones and some gold, almost eight thousand American Dollars, but now looking at them there was no question that the expense was well justified.

The dress was next and it went on like a glove. Claire had decided to wear five-inch heels that matched the dress. She had had to get them special ordered from New York and had them overnighted, but the agency was picking up the tab, so who cared? Finally she chose her coat. Claire had bought three Givenchy furs over the years. The newest one was a white floor length mink with black mink outer lining and satin inner lining. The stark white of the coat set off her hair as blood on snow. That was an image that Rachel chose not to pass on to the world's newest diva.

"Gentlemen," Rachel shouted from the second floor landing, "I present to you Miss Claire Daniels." All eyes turned to the stairs as Claire descended, the fur buttoned.

Stepping off the stairs into the hallway the red head turned twice in the coat. Then as if on the runway of Milan, she unbuttoned the coat and let it drop off her shoulders. The effect was stunning. The emerald green dress seemed to escape from the coat. Claire stood there amid the hoots and whistles of her companions. She wouldn't admit it but inwardly she was very pleased at the effect. Finally feeling self-conscious she pulled the coat back on, and walked toward the door.

"Oh, by the way," Frack said from the archway to the kitchen, "Michael called while you were getting ready. "He said to pull up to the front doors. He's going to block out a space for us by his Rolls." Frack noticed the reaction to the word Rolls. Everyone perked up their ears.

"Do we know what this guy looks like?" Claire asked.

"Here's a photo of him and his wife at a fund raiser last year." Frack handed Claire a printout of a newspaper photo. It showed a tall, older man with full gray hair standing next to a stunning brunette. The caption said Melissa and Michael Bishop at the Weirs Beach Fund Run.

"Six-thirty," Rachel said, "time to hit the trail." Leaving Frick and Frack at the farmhouse the four others climbed into the SUV, the men helping their female counterparts into the back seat.

"Are you armed?" Myer said to Claire.

"You've got to be kidding." Claire was aghast. "I don't have enough room in this dress for what I have, forget something extra."

The drive to Laconia was uneventful. Laconia is one of the most beautiful lake towns in New England. Lake Winnipesaukee covers an area the size of some small towns and offers boating, fishing, water skiing, swimming, and other summer and winter sports. From a number of different vantage points the lake spreads out like a blue carpet set in the tree lined valley of the town proper. Just before coming into the suburbs of the city the SUV received a call from the farmhouse.

"Mobile, this is base." Frick's voice came through loud and clear. "Our visitor is back."

"Base this is mobile." Myer took the radio, while Mac drove. "We copy. Any change from last night?"

"Negative mobile. Same place."

"Keep us apprised." Myer said. "Mobile out."

"I'd sure like to know who she is." Mac shouted over the road noise.

"She must have gotten there after we left." Rachel leaned over the front seat. "Probably thinks we're still in the house."

"If she's still there when we get back, we can go through the mud room." Claire looked out the window at the houses and empty fields. "From where she is she won't be able to get a shot off, if that's her intention."

With two more turns the black van was slowing down into the left turn lane. Claire looked through the windshield to see a large parking lot in front of a dark green building. Passing by the sign at the turn she read 'CLAIRE DANIELS APPEARING TONIGHT LIVE WITH THE WHITE MOUNTAIN BOYS' and her stomach turned again.

"I think I'm going to puke." She said to no one in particular.

"Not in that coat you don't" Rachel said sternly. "Take a deep breath and suck it up. Tonight you're the star of the show. Now," opening her van door and talking the hand of the valet, "act it!"

Claire took a couple of deep breaths of cold mountain air as her door was opened by a young valet in black tails and stepped onto the asphalt on shaky legs. She scanned the parking lot and noticed there wasn't a single empty space. Turning to Mac, at her side she asked.

"How many cars do you count?" Claire whispered.

"Must be over three hundred." Mac said.

"Shit." Claire said with a smile, since she had entered the lights of the front foyer.

Suddenly Michael was in front of her, hugging her. "My God, girl, you get more beautiful every time I see you. And firm." He hugged her again. "My wife would kill to have your figure at her age." Looking down the front opening of her coat he smiled. "And your breasts are still magnificent."

Uhuh, thought Rachel, here it comes.

Instead Claire smiled and said "Thank you Michael, you're always so kind." Turning to the black woman standing next to her she said. "This is my best friend Rachel Jackson." Michael reached out and, before Rachel could side step the big man, he had picked her up off the ground with a hug.

"Welcome Claire's best friend Rachel." He laughed deeply.

"And these are our escorts, Chris and Brian." Claire waved her hand to Mac and Myer.

Instead of a hug Michael had his hand out shaking theirs until Myer thought his would fall off. The old guy had a grip like a vice.

"Welcome to all of you." He almost pushed the crowd into the front doors. "We thought we'd have a little party for your return. Just a few friends." He stopped everyone before a giant set of red leather tufted doors made of mahogany and brass. "Is everyone ready?" Looking at the four guests.

Claire took another deep breath and wanted to head for the exit. Instead she unbuttoned her fur. Michael reached for a cordless microphone, turned it on and began shouting at the top of his lungs.

"Ladies and gentlemen." The loudspeaker boomed his voice all over the building, and in the small entryway, the sound was crushing. "It is my personal pleasure to present after a much too long absence, Claire Daniels."

Opening the doors to the club, a set of white lights struck Claire full force. Rachel and the boys were momentarily blinded, but Claire walked into the spots, and following Michael, entered the bar. As if rehearsed she opened the white mink at the halfway point and the audience exploded with applause. Rachel looked from side to side and thought that there must be at least five hundred people in the room. No wonder, she thought, he could afford a Rolls. At ten dollars a head he had five grand just in door receipts.

Michael led the four to a ringside table where his wife was already sitting. She gave her friend a hug and greeted the others. Mac and Myer took opposite sides of the table and started setting up the remote video equipment. Fitting in a briefcase the setup could send a digital color image back to the farmhouse in real time. Frick had wired the wide screen television in the library to carry the broadcast so they could watch the show. Unknown to those in Laconia, he was also recording everything in case something happened.

A waiter came and took their drink order and carried away their jackets and coats. Claire ordered a Shirley Temple, double cherry, no ice, Rachel had a Perrier with lime, Mac had a Mississippi Highball, which meant ice water, and Myer drank a Dr. Pepper. After a few minutes to give the crowd a chance to settle down Michael got up on the stage and put his mike in the stand.

"Friends," he started talking slowly and quietly over the crowd noises, "we were all sorry to hear about Claire's accident last year. I know a lot of you expressed concern when the papers said she might not live, but she's tougher than they thought." Looking down at the group in front of him. "I'd like to ask Claire to join me on stage and maybe we can beg her to sing a song or two." The audience started to clap. Michael, reaching his hand out to the girl, still sitting, motioned her to him.

"Give em Hell." Said Mac.

"We got faith in you." Whispered Myer.

"It's now or never." Smiled Rachel.

Claire got up and slowly walked to the stage. The clapping had gotten louder, and she could feel the stage vibrate from the applause. Taking her hand, Michael helped her onto the stage. The light from all the spots threw green sparkles throughout the room.

Back at the library in Laconia, the video feed made the stage look like Madison Square Garden. Frick and Frack had made popcorn, and with beer in hand, sat back to watch the show. Next to them on the end table was a small monitor, still showing one red dot, two hundred yards from the north wall of the house.

Claire handed a small note to the guitar player. He looked down at it and then back up to her. With a grin he nodded his head and handed the note around to the other three members of the band. The other guitar player smiled as soon as he looked at the paper. So it was with the bass player and the girl with long blonde hair playing drums. Claire turned back to the mike and cleared her throat.

"I'd like to thank Michael for this night." She looked out over a sea of faces. "I never expected so many people for a local band and a Karaoke singer." At that the crowd let loose another round of cheers and laughter. "Michael," she looked at the older man leaving the stage, "I hope that tonight has not been a mistake." Looking back at the audience. "I had a small accident last year." She looked at her shoes. "My lung was damaged and sometimes breathing is a little difficult."

Rachel leaned over to Myer and whispered in his ear. "I think this is her way of explaining if she can't hold a tune."

"Anyway." Claire went on. "I hope you're not disappointed by tonight. And I'll say this now, in case I have to run from the tomatoes being thrown at the end of the night, once again, thank you for being here."

She winked once to Rachel. Blew a kiss to Mac and Myer and turned her back on the audience. As the lights went down across the bar she quietly told the band. "Start with number one and keep going. I'll let you know if I want to stop." She smiled at the band, knowing that they had never met before, and for one brief night, were going to try to keep five hundred people from stampeding the doors in fright. "Hit it."

The guitars started with 'Why Haven't I Heard From You." From there Claire went through all the major Reba hits and then some of her lesser known ones. She sang softly, hard, sweet and clear. By the third number the waiters stopped refilling drinks. No one was drinking. The waitresses stopped taking food orders, the cooks and dish staff stood by the kitchen doors. Other than the girl on the stage, there wasn't another sound in the entire building. When the singles were exhausted the drummer and the red head did the Linda Davis, Reba duets. Finally the two guitar players and Claire did the Brooks and Dunn, Reba number one hit If You See Him, If You See Her. She sang for seventy minutes: no break, no water. Finally she ended with I'd Rather Ride Around With You and dropped her head.

After a few seconds, sweaty and tired she looked up into the lights. There wasn't a sound anywhere. She thought that if she ran quickly she could get to the door before anyone noticed, but then Rachel, Mac and Myer started to clap, then a few more, then the entire crowd were on their feet screaming. The lights came up over an ocean of satisfied faces, beating beer bottles on the tables and cheering as loudly as they could. That's when it struck the lone singer on stage that she had done better than she ever could have imagined.

Michael joined Claire shortly after that thought. He put his arm around her waist and held the other in the air. The applause continued until he motioned the crowd to please sit. Speaking into the mike he said.

"If we're real nice, maybe Claire will do something else later.

Would you like that?" More applause. "Let's give the band a hand also for this incredible performance." More clapping and cheering. The lights went off on the stage and Michael helped his star to her seat.

"Bathroom." Claire said to Rachel.

"You can use the one in the office." Melissa pointed to a door at the back of the stage.

Rachel and Claire, with Mac in tow to stand guard headed for the back room. Once alone in the small bathroom Rachel couldn't contain herself anymore.

"Don't you ever fuckin' tell me you can't sing again." Rachel was all grins.

"Was it okay?" Claire had to pee; and she didn't care if someone else was in the room.

"I think the crowd answered that for you. I thought you said you couldn't sing?"

"It just happened." Claire stood back up and adjusted herself. Wiping sweat off her chest with a towel she looked at her closest friend. "One more time, please. Was it okay?"

Rachel hugged her and she almost started crying. "Claire it was the best night I have ever had."

"You need to get out more." Claire shot back, and the two broke down laughing.

Rejoining the others at the table, Claire had at least fifteen Shirley Temples in front of her. Melissa said most were from men, but with a wink, some were from ladies. Peter, the lead guitarist from the band came over to thank Claire for the set.

"That was amazing." He gushed. "If you ever want to go on the road, please let us know. We'll quit our day jobs for you."

Claire laughed at the compliment. She grabbed a napkin and a pen from Myer and wrote some notes on the paper. "Do you guys know these?" She handed the napkin to Peter.

"I knew there was something I liked about you other than your looks, your voice, and your dress. Whenever you're ready."

"Give me some time to rest and then we'll try again." Claire went to shake Peter's hand but he took it and kissed it lightly. Turning quickly he was swallowed up by the crowd.

"Frick says the feed was crystal clear," Mac said to Rachel and Claire and in a lower tone, "also our visitor hasn't moved."

The talk flowed freely throughout the table. Michael told stories about Claire, from before the shooting. Claire laughed more at the way he told the stories than the stories themselves. Danny had never heard any of these incidents, which were mostly off color or physical in nature. It seemed that Claire had a streak of mischief that often led to her being confronted for her sins. It was evident to everyone at the table that there was a deep love and respect for Claire from Michael and Melissa.

Claire finally cooled down and stopped perspiring. She looked at the large room and noticed that no one had left. She wondered if they were all waiting for another set from her. The band had been warming up with some top forty-cover songs and when she looked at the stage Peter gave her a nod and a questioning look. Smiling back at him she nodded and finished her drink.

"I think it's time to do it again." She smiled at Michael. "With your permission."

Michael started to get up but a slender white arm reached over and stopped him. "It's okay." Claire said. "Let me do this one myself."

Claire stepped up onto the stage. The lights dimmed for the second time and a single spot lit her microphone stand. She again looked out into the audience and smiled.

"Thank you for the warm reception earlier." She started. "I know that you came to hear country, but I'd like to do something a little different this time. My best friend Rachel, who by the way is single, she saw Rachel bury her head in her hands, accuses me of being two different people. I guess that's true sometimes because I'm not always boots and jeans." She spread out her arms and twirled in the light. "I also clean up real good for show." There was a wave of laughter from the audience.

Continuing. "Growing up I always wanted to be a forties torch singer. This is my offering to those greats of past years. Gentlemen,

103

if you will."

The audience didn't know what to expect when Claire started singing. She began with God Bless the Child as Billy Holiday had performed it. She moved on, then, through the show tunes to include Summertime from Porgy and Bess, and Handbags and Glad rags. She kept the set short this time, singing for about forty-five minutes. At the end the reaction was the same. The crowd took to the venue with increased admiration. Claire stood in the limelight and soaked up the first positive emotions she had received since the shooting. She wouldn't want to do this for a living, she thought, but it sure beat getting shot.

Claire walked off the stage in a fog. She had done two sets in front of at least five hundred people and they had liked her. Rejoining her tablemates she had a grin from ear to ear. "That," she said sitting down, "is real music."

After another trip to the ladies room and with Rachel in tow Claire made the rounds of the bar. Everyone seemed to know her and they all were genuinely glad she was all right. Claire was gaining new respect for her cousin. Danny never would have thought that the workaholic that he ate Sunday dinner with every week was so popular with so many diverse people. The facets of Claire Daniels seemed never ending, however, the night was. She noticed Mac breaking down the equipment on the table when the girls returned. Looking at Michael's wristwatch she was surprised to see that it was already after one in the morning. She felt as if she could go on all night, but the others had a different picture. Appearing with the coats Myer held the white fur for Claire.

"Time to go home Princess." Rachel said, getting an assist from Mac with her jacket.

"It was a magical night, wasn't it?" She snuggled into the cool fur.

One last hug by Michael and Melissa and the four were out the doors. The wind blew cold from the north across the parking lot. Claire wondered if the planting was underway back in the Falls. That thought, more than the weather, made her shiver to the bone and she hurriedly got into the front seat of the SUV. Once out of the parking lot and onto the road north she took the radio and called base.

"Base this is mobile." Claire waited for an answer.

"This is base." It was Frick. "Is this the world famous Claire Daniels, star extraordinaire?"

"Cute base." Claire couldn't help but smile. "What's the situation?"

"No change." Frick said. "Contact is still there."

"Are we certain it's a human body and not some kind of decoy?" Asked Claire

"Affirmative." Replied Frick. "I can see her complete silhouette. No doubt it's a real person. What's your twenty?"

"Twenty in less than an hour." Claire expected to arrive at the farmhouse about two thirty in the morning. "Mobile out."

"I was thinking." Mac said, still driving north. "If I drive in the yard from the other side it should put my headlights into that section of field that the girl is using. And, if I had on my high beams when we made the turn she wouldn't even think that there was anything out of the ordinary. We might even get a glimpse of her on the attic cam."

"I could kiss you balding head for that." Claire was definitely out of character tonight. "Base this is mobile." She grabbed the radio.

"Go ahead mobile." Frack answered this time.

"We're going to try to get some light on our visitor. Get the attic camera aligned to her direction and start the recorder. Mac is going to try to hit her with the headlights on the drive up to the house. Do you copy, over?"

"We copy mobile."

"Mobile out."

A few minutes later Mac, driving the SUV very slowly up the driveway, succeeded in illuminating the girl for a split second before she ran for deep cover. No one in the van could tell much bouncing up the driveway, but the camera in the attic window got a full five seconds on tape.

Pulling the van around the other side of the farmhouse the four agents entered through the mudroom into the kitchen.

"Did you get her?" Claire hadn't even taken off her coat.

"Yes ma'am. Got a good three second burst." Frick was already rewinding the tape.

Still in heels and her green dress Claire stood over Frick as he ran the tape. Rachel thought the scene the ultimate in surreal; Claire in five inch heels, her breasts almost touching the older agents head, looking down at the video.

Frick ran the video at half speed. Everyone could see the lights sweep around through the field and strike a young woman of about twenty wearing a dark green field jacket and blue jeans. She had a black baseball cap on with a long ponytail of black hair pulled through the hole in the back. As soon as the light struck her she was up and out of the frame.

Fatigue finally struck as Rachel and Claire turned away from the video. Not letting anyone else see how tired she was Claire called everyone into the room and gave the nights orders.

"I doubt the girl will be back tonight" she started, "however I don't want to take the chance. Keep the sensors up all around the farm. I'm guessing that since she was spotted in one place she'll try for another one. Whoever she is, there's something of interest in here."

"Before everyone else goes to bed, and leave us here to watch heat signatures," Frack was playing for sympathy, "I have a gift for you all." He started handing out plastic DVD cases. On the cover was a still of Claire on stage at Michael's bar. "This is the DVD of the show tonight. I burned a copy for each of us as a memory." Handing a Sharpie marker to Claire he asked. "Would you autograph my copy please."

Claire smiled as she signed everybody's copy. This really was her family now for better or for worse, just like real families.

"I'm going to bed." Claire headed upstairs. "Tomorrow afternoon we try the key. Figure out who goes caving with me."

Rachel came out of the kitchen to follow Claire. In her arms she had a bottle of Moxie, a can of Diet Coke and the tin of Crisco from under the counter.

When the girls got to the third floor, they immediately stripped and tossed all their clothes in the hamper. They each smelled like smoke, something which neither appreciated. Now wearing just briefs they met in the bathroom.

"What's with the Crisco?" Claire reached for the soap to clean her face.

Grabbing the bar away from her, Rachel slapped a gob of Crisco in Claire's hand. "Use this instead." Rachel began applying it all over her face. "Works much better than anything on the market, it's cheap, and doesn't have any smell to it."

"Where'd you learn this trick?" Claire was amazed at how easily the makeup wiped off her face.

"Acting classes in college." Rachel finished her face. "We had a professor named Dr. White. This guy knew everything about the theatre. Worked us like dogs, but I learned more about makeup and construction from him than from anyone else alive or dead. This trick came when I played Christine in We're No Angels, you know the play version of the movie Bogart and Aldo Rey did." Rachel started laughing.

"What's so funny?" They headed back down the hall.

"I was a little heavier then," Rachel turned into her room and stopped at the door, "and the kid that was supposed to carry me across the stage was a good thirty pounds lighter than me. He had to hold me in his arms and say 'She's light as a feather.' Every night I expected him to drop me on my ass."

Looking straight into Claire's eyes Rachel said. "You did good tonight. We were very proud of you, especially me." At that Rachel went to bed.

Claire turned into her room before she started to cry. She crawled under the heavy blankets and smiled until she fell asleep.

0400 hours, 20 May 2001

Myer watched the heat signature move across the east side of the farm property. From where the visitor now was, Myer estimated she was seventy-five yards behind the barn. There was no line of sight to the house from there so he figured she'd work her way around one side of the barn. Instead the red dot remained in place for a few minutes and then disappeared off screen. Reappearing the dot quickly left the sensor area. Myer made a note on the event log to look out behind the barn in the morning.

CHAPTER EIGHT

The clouds finally broke at dawn. The sun rose over a foggy, but warmer valley, and the farmhouse was bathed in a golden glow. By ten everyone was up and at their chores. Frick was already in the basement firing pistol rounds into a slab of ribs. Claire had failed to mention his project, not wanting the others to get their hopes up on the outcome. If what happened in the basement worked then they would have a better chance against both the tall man and Steve.

Myer was out behind the barn looking for why their visitor had disappeared from the heat sensors for a few moments. He thought that the entrance to the mythical tunnel might be in the underbrush. Instead all he found was some broken branches where it looked as though the girl had fallen into the river. If that were the case, then the cold water would have cancelled out enough heat from her body to make it look like she disappeared. Not taking any chances he continued scouring every square foot of the area until almost noon.

Mac was going from room to room laying out equipment for the internal camera system. Even though the system was tied into the power of the farmhouse, he was providing backup in case the power grid failed. In another two days it should be ready to install in the walls and ceiling.

It was decided that Frack go with the girls. He volunteered, when he heard there might be a chance to see uncharted underground caves. Growing up in New Mexico he had caved in all the major ones, and had been responsible for some new finds. His father had free climbed with the famous Warren 'Batso' Harding and had passed the trait of take it in take it back out to his son.

Rachel and Claire dressed for a long day underground. They had lights, water, food, radios, rope, snaps, carabineers, and chocks. They had even ordered helmets from the agency when they realized that the caves might be more extensive than a few mere tunnels. Rachel had told Claire she was going to be very disappointed if the door opened to a broom closet.

After lunch the three piled into the SUV and drove to the library. Claire felt like a scene from Ghostbusters, equipment clanking on their hips, walking through an empty library, and into the lower level.

Miss Carter was sitting at her desk when the three entered the room. She looked up from her desk, smiled and said. "After such a night as you had, you have the energy to explore?"

"You know about last night?" Claire was taken back at the woman's reach of information.

"I was just reading about it." She held out a section of newspaper. "See, they got a nice picture of you."

Claire took the issue, and with Rachel and Frack peering over her shoulders saw a photo of her on stage at Michaels. The caption said 'Claire Daniels, local historian and singer, entertains at No Secrets Friday night. Performing both country and blues Miss Daniels kept the crowd, estimated at over six hundred, enthralled all night.' The photo credit was M. Carter. The paper was the Laconia Citizen.

Handing the paper back to the librarian Claire asked. "M. Carter? A relative?"

"My great niece, Manda." Miss Carter said. "Right fine newsgirl. Edits the entertainment section." The old lady folded the newspaper and put it in a bin behind her. "She had it sent special this morning so I could read all about you."

"You're a rock star after all." Rachel poked Claire in the ribs.

"Going back to look for Daryl?" Hester asked.

"No ma'am. Going to look past the big wooden door." Claire held up her key. "I found the key the other day."

Hester gave a little frown and shook her head. "Don't know what that key fits, but it ain't the door at the end of the tunnels."

Claire was crestfallen. She had convinced herself that the key from her dreams was the answer to the riddle.

Instead, Miss Carter opened a drawer in her desk and pulled out a bigger older key than Claire's "This is the key for the door." She handed it to Claire. "Take good care of it. It's the only one."

Claire thanked the librarian for the help and promised to return the key when they were done. Taking the lead she stuck off through the back doors and into the tunnels. Retracing their steps from the last time they came to the door. Frack turned the key in the lock and the great door swung open. Closing the lock on the hasp to keep anyone from locking them in the three entered the tunnel.

There was no outstanding change from one side of the door to the other. The tunnel continued with no forks or turns. For what seemed like days, although it was only twenty-five minutes, the three started hearing noises up ahead. At first it sounded like the wind, but Rachel doubted that the wind was coming in through the tunnel. Frack said it reminded him of a train bearing down on them, but again a train seemed unlikely. Finally they all realized the sound was falling water and before they could verbalize that discovery to each other they entered a vast cavern, and stepped into a puddle.

Backing up a step they looked down to see water seeping onto the floor. Pulling a mini-halogen floodlight from his pack, Frack turned it on. The view was awe-inspiring. The cavern was only about thirty feet high, but spread out for what looked like a thousand feet in any direction. The sound of falling water was indeed that: a waterfall on one side, falling from the ceiling to a pool below. It was half way down the right side of the cavern. In the center of the opening the water had carved a riverbed before running out the other end and into the opposite wall. Walking to the bank of the river, through the mud and puddles Rachel pointed to something.

"Over there." She yelled at Frack, over the sound of the water.

Shining the light in the direction of Rachel's pointed arm the three saw what looked like a skeleton. Walking quickly to the spot the girls and Frack stood over the body. The bones were intact, lying at an eddy in the river. There was no flesh on the body, but the hair was still attached and looked to have been long and brown. Rachel bent over and saw on one finger was a girl's school ring from Fryeburg Academy.

"I wonder who she was and how she got here?" Rachel stood

back up.

"Her name was Kathy Robbins. She drowned in 1954 at the base of Carter Falls." Claire looked down at the bones, trying to think what the Robbins girl might have looked like.

"Is this another vision of yours?" Rachel was getting real tired of prophetic dreams and visions, especially her own, but at least Claire's were coming true.

"No, it's in another issue of 'Unnatural Horror' magazine. I read it the other night while looking for clues about the key.

"So we're right below the infamous Carter Falls?" Frack looked up.

"What is it with these falls?" Rachel asked. "I thought they were just the name of the town."

"Oh hell no." Claire corrected her friend. "The Falls used to be in the middle of a large stand of trees, far from civilization. As kids everyone from around here used to dare each other to swim there after dark. No one ever thought that there was any danger, it was just a great place to go, away from the eyes of the adults." Also looking up to the ceiling of the cavern. "Looks like there's an opening to the surface, through the rocks. The body must have been caught in the pull and sucked under." Claire turned toward the tunnel they came in through. "We must leave quickly." She said with urgency. "Don't ask questions, just follow me."

Almost running Claire covered the three hundred meters in less than a minute. Rachel and Frack had a hard time keeping up with the red head and they clinked and clanked down the tunnel, back to the wooden door. It only took fifteen minutes to reach the doorway, and once all three were through, Claire unlocked the great pad lock and relocked the door. Only then did she slow down.

"What was that all about?" Rachel was breathing heavy from the run and Frack was leaning against the tunnel wall gasping.

"I'll let you read the rest of the story." Claire slowly started walking back to the library. "You may say so what, but I think that 'Unnatural Horror' magazine may be the answer to many of our questions."

When the three returned to the library basement Miss Carter was still sitting at her desk. Claire wondered if she ever moved, or had a home, other than this room.

"Miss Carter," Claire went up to the librarian's desk, "we're going to have to get someone down here from the State Police. We found a body beyond the wooden door."

Hester Carter acted as though it were just another request for a book when she answered. "Do you know how she died?" Miss Carter said. "You cannot move the body. There are far more terrible things underground than the dead."

"You mean the sacrifice?" Claire asked.

"What sacrifice?" Rachel interrupted.

"Billy was my cousin Heidi's boy." Hester said. "Ain't right the way he died. Never heard the whole thing, just what we read in the papers, until the story came out. After that the other three went away. Wouldn't even talk to the police."

"There were six that night." Claire pressed. "What happened to the one who wrote the story? There was no author listed."

"Don't know who he was. Might not even be a he." Miss Carter said with a sigh. "This town has a lot of secrets. Some you can discover, some discover you."

Claire laid the key on the desk and started to leave.

"You gonna take the body?" Hester asked slowly.

"No ma'am." Claire started up the stairs. "But we'll be back."

The three tired adventurers walked out of the library and into the setting sunlight. Claire pushed Frack into the passenger seat and took the wheel. Frack didn't care at that point. He was just happy to be sitting on something soft. His feet hurt, he was hungry, and he wanted to know what the hell was going on.

The farmhouse was north of the town square, but Claire turned the SUV east and headed out. After a few minutes she turned onto a newly paved road and then into a secluded housing development, still under construction. The houses being built were four to six bedroom capes with landscaped yards and three car garages. Driving the van through a set of large double iron gates they entered the

Carter Falls Municipal Golf Course and Country Club. Pulling up to the clubhouse she ordered everyone out. As she walked into the pro shop she pulled out an FBI identification badge and showed it to the kid behind the counter.

"We need to use two of your golf carts for about an hour." Claire smiled demurely.

"Yes ma'am." The young boy stuttered. "Take which ever ones you want. Anything else I can do?"

"No, thank you." Claire again took the lead and the three got into two carts; Frack driving with Rachel, and Claire leading the way down the path as the light was starting to dim. The golf course was still under construction, but the two or three holes that they could still see in the light looked gorgeous. Claire had never golfed before but thought it might be a nice way to exercise. You could smell the green grass, see birds and small animals running around, and take a nice walk for four hours. The two carts pulled up to a tee and everyone got out.

The sound of falling water was again in the air. Claire led the other two down the gravel path to a pristine green and then around a sand bunker. When she stopped the group was standing in front of a massive rock outcropping, at least a hundred feet high, with water pouring out of the top and splashing into a large pool eight to ten feet below them.

"This is Carter's Fall." Claire pointed to the water. "At one time this was all forest. It used to take us an hour to walk here through the paths that had been beaten into the ground. There was a tradition that if you lost your virginity here you threw a silver dollar into the pool and wished for another one."

"Where does the water go?" Asked Frack.

"There's a small creek behind the falls that leads to the river behind our farm." Claire sat on the grass in the first cut. "I never thought about the water before, but there was always so much coming out of the Falls and so little going into the creek. Make's you wonder if the architects that built the course knew about the tunnels."

"What was so important that an entire town was named after the waterfall?" Rachel sat next to Claire, and Frack next to Rachel. The air was clear and cool and the sound of the falling water was soothing.

"I don't know." Claire turned to look at the other two. "The notes in my room say that the town was originally called New Hancock. Then later on it was changed to Carter's Fall and finally to Carter Falls."

Standing up she said to the two sitting. "Let's go back to the farmhouse. I want you to read why we left the tunnels, and I need a suggestion on where to go from here."

The cart ride back was slower, since the slightly less than full moon only lighted the course. Returning the carts they drove back to the farmhouse in silence.

When they got into the house the smell of stew pulled them to the kitchen. Mac had made a great beef stock on the stove, and had vegetables and large chunks of meat floating in the brown sauce. He had also baked a loaf of bread, something that Myer and Frick kept ribbing him about. The three from the tunnels washed and sat at the dining table with their friends.

"What's the occasion?" Rachel asked. "I didn't expect Susie Homemaker when I got back."

"The tests were very positive." Frick said. "Mac decided to celebrate and he went crazy in the kitchen."

As they ate Claire had Frick explain what he had been doing in the basement all day.

"Claire wanted to see if there was a way of being bullet proof without being bulky." Frick started. "The new woven Kevlar is now being used as a T shirt with limited success. It won't stop a large caliber, but stops up to a twenty five round." Frick took another bite of gravy soaked bread. "Anyway, we thought that if we used more than one layer the stop ability might increase."

"And did it?" Frack was curious.

"Sure did. Using three shirts you should survive a 7.62x25 round." Frick pushed his bowl away from him.

"I am assuming," Claire, said, "unless someone else has a better idea, that Steve will continue to use the CZ-52. I am also assuming that if we can push the tall man to attack us here he will also use the CZ and try to blame the slaughter on Steve." Claire looked around the table at five sets of eyes. "We just have to figure out how to make him shoot us wearing the shirts."

After dinner Claire went upstairs and brought back another worn issue of 'Unnatural Horror' magazine. She handed it to Rachel who didn't question the reason this time. When she finished it she passed it to Frack. The story was short with no author credit.

A NIGHT AT THE FALLS

No one goes to the Falls much anymore. When we were kids, however, the Falls was the place to go on hot afternoons. There were six of us then: Robert Carter, his cousins Glenn and Dave, William Dunlary, Kathy Robbins and myself. We were all eighteen; a young age, I now realize, for what was about to happen that summer.

School got out that year the seventh of June. Within a week the temperature had climbed to 94 degrees and the Carter Falls Slip and Slide Club was formed. We swam every day with the younger kids and then late at night we'd strip and skinny dip.

The summer flew by, at least to us. In August we planned on celebrating the full moon with a sacrifice. Kathy was the closest thing we had to a virgin so she was elected. Billy had found some old yarn and a rusty tent peg to use. These two things, and some charcoal from an old barbecue, were what he was going to use to call up the 'evil ones' as he called them.

The night of the 'sacrifice' we met at the beach just before ten. Kathy fought with mock fright as she was bound hand and foot with the yarn and then lifted onto the picnic table at the waters edge. We stood around, with the full moon to Billy's back, waiting to begin. Billy marked a pentagram on Kathy's stomach and placed some odd signs around the outside of it. Holding the tent peg he invoked the names of Hastur and Yog'Sothoth.

Perhaps we should have felt the vibrations. The rushing of the Falls, I believe, is why we were not aware of what was happening.

Billy and Dave picked Kathy up and threw her off our diving rock into the deepest part of the pool. It had been the plan for her to emerge from the water cleansed and looking like Venus emerging from the Sea.

It was Glenn that called our attention to the glow, even before Kathy hit the water. Under the Falls the light was bright orange; spreading into a deep red out into the pool. The vibrations began to shake the rocks beneath us as we waited for Kathy to surface. After a couple of minutes Billy began to get scared and dove into the red water, still holding the tent peg.

No one swims much at the Falls anymore, since they found Billy the next morning. The state police brought him up in their nets. The tent peg he had used for his sacrificial knife was buried deep into his chest. Two of the officers fainted when they saw him. All the others went to the bushes to vomit.

All of them had at one time or another seen a corpse but this one was different. Billy's skin had been removed, more accurately Billy had been turned inside out, with his skeleton and organs wrapped around it.

Kathy's body was never found. Whatever it had been that had skinned Billy must have liked its other offering better. That was fourteen years ago and no one goes to the Falls much anymore.

After everyone else read the story they each, in their own way, gave Claire 'that look'. Claire merely sat back at the dining table and looked back at them. "Well?" She asked. "Don't look at me like that. I didn't stick the girl in the cavern."

"Is this where someone is supposed to go to the kitchen and say 'I'll be right back' then gets murdered?" Myer wasn't trying to be funny.

"No, this is where we sit here and figure out how to kill Steve, stop the tall man, and find out if there is anything else in the tunnels." Claire was playing with a fork.

"You know." Mac said. "Just when I think this fucking town can't get any weirder something proves me wrong." He stared out the window into the darkness. "When I was a kid I was afraid of the dark. My dad gave me the same bullshit we all tell kids, that there's nothing in the dark that can hurt you. You know, when you close your eyes its dark, and all that crap." He looked back at the group. "I've seen people get killed in the dark, run off the road, drive into things, fall, I know damned well the dark can hurt you. I also knew that there were no such things as monsters, except the human kind that kill for pleasure or money or sport." Mac closed his eyes and rubbed the bridge of his nose. "Now I'm not so sure about any of what I knew."

"I forgot to tell you." Myer said to Rachel. "Someone named Rodriguez called while you were out. Said to send the packet to Susan's apartment by certified mail." Does that make sense?"

Rachel's entire demeanor changed. She brightened up and clapped her hands in front of her. "It sure does. Susan was my roommate when I started at the agency. Her father is my immediate boss, the one that Avery had to call to get me on this case. I sent him an encrypted email this morning telling him what we thought and could I use him as a safe drop." Rachel popped out of her chair. "We now have an out if this goes badly." She started piling papers from the conference room together. "Manny will see to it that the proper authorities see this."

"All right then," Claire picked up her plate and silver wear, "let's get the table cleared and wash up. Things are starting to look better."

At eleven-thirty Frick stuck his head into Claire's room and told her that the visitor was back.

"Tell everyone I want lights out slowly by midnight." Claire changed out of her nightdress and into a denim skirt and long sleeve T. Her shoulder holster bunched the shirt at the armpits but it also pulled the shirt tight across her chest, making her look heavier than she actually was. At twelve-twenty they were all gathered around the monitor in the conference room, watching the single red light in the tree line.

"Bring her in." Claire said flatly.

Myer and Frick started moving to the mudroom door.

"What if she has other ideas?" Frick asked.

"Don't kill her." Claire returned. "Other than that, bring her here." Now four sets of eyes watched the monitor. They could see the two red dots, which were Frick and Myer, move in a flanking action around both sides of the stationary target. Coming up behind the girl the three dots converged into one. After a moment the single, large dot began moving back to the house, through the open field.

Even before the three came into the house, Claire could hear the girl screaming across the landscape.

"Let go of me you animal." She yelled as she was dragged into the conference room. "I'll see all of you in jail by tomorrow morning. Nobody grabs me a gets away with it."

Myer threw the girl onto the floor at Claire and Rachel's feet.

Before the girl could regain her footing, Claire drove her boot heel into the girl's chest, driving the shoulders and head back to the wooden floor.

"You're very wrong little girl." Claire looked down. "We can grab you and get away with it any time we like. Who are you?" Claire was going for all the meanness she could muster.

"Fuck you." The girl spat back.

Claire put more weight on her heel and it bit deeper into the girls skin through the army jacket. "This is your last chance." Claire said. "Who are you?"

"You killed my brother." The girls screamed. "You shot him in the back like an animal.

The room finally realized the connection to the girl. Here was the sister to one of the three that Steve had killed the other night on Snowville Pond Road.

"Listen to me very carefully." Claire bent over to look the girl in the eyes. "I didn't kill your brother. He and his friends tried to run my friend and I off the road so we helped him into Snowville Pond. Your brother was killed after he came out of the water by someone who would have already killed you by now if he were here." She couldn't tell if she was getting through to the scared little girl.

"I'll make you all pay." Evidently Claire had failed. "There are laws. You can't get away with this. I'll go to the police."

"I could shoot you right now and dump your body in the driveway of the State Police barracks in Moultonborough and no one would do anything about it. We are the police." Claire was getting tired of this.

"Screw it. Frick, Frack, take her out to the dry well, shoot her and dump her in."

Immediately the two agents each grabbed one of the girls kicking legs and started dragging her out of the house.

"You can't do this." The girl was getting hysterical. She grabbed onto the door jam to the living room.

Claire walked over to her, took her heel and kicked the girl's fingers and smiled. "I can do anything I want. Now do you want to answer questions or die?"

"My name is Denise Butler." The girl on the floor began to cry.

"Now Denise." Claire helped her to a chair. "What did you expect to accomplish spying on us every night from the tree line?"

"You knew I was there?" Denise tried to stop crying.

"From the first moment you appeared." Rachel tossed the girl a hankie. "Would you like something to drink?"

She nodded and Rachel sent Mac for a glass of water.

"Was your brother the one driving?" Claire pulled up a chair next to the girl. Mac brought the water and Denise drained it before speaking.

"Yes"

"I broke his nose last year, but I didn't kill him." Claire replied. "He was killed by someone who is trying to kill all of us. Your brother and his friends were killed because they got in the way."

In another hour the girl was calm enough to be allowed to leave. She walked out the front door and across the field. Her red dot continued in a straight line until it went off the screen. At that point the farmhouse went to bed for the second time that night.

"Do you think she'll be back?" Questioned Rachel, as they went up the stairs.

"Don't know." Claire replied. "I couldn't just shoot her."

"The real Claire would have." Came back the unexpected answer.
"Yea, I know." Claire turned into her room and shut the door.

CHAPTER NINE

May 22, 2001

There were no nightly visitors this time. The shifts ran through their routines without disturbance, and those that were not on shift slept soundly. In the morning, everyone was alert and unusually perky. The weather that had plagued them for so long had finally vanished, leaving the valley, and the farmhouse in glorious light. The boys saw Rachel on the back porch drawing the front of the barn in some charcoals that she had found in the library. She wasn't that good at what she was doing, but it beat sitting around and waiting for the next strange shoe to fall.

Claire was on the front porch, not drawing, but reading. She had found more issues of 'Unnatural Horror' magazine in a closet, and was browsing them for anything interesting. For some reason her cousin had believed that these issues held some kind of key to the mystery, or else why would she have kept them?

Rachel got bored first and came looking for Claire. Rachel was surprised at how close the two had become in the last months. Their differences were not just obvious, the ethnic and cultural ones, their philosophies on life differed radically at times. Rachel was very scientific, which assisted her in getting through medical school and into the agency. Claire, when she was Danny, had operated more on instinct. Even now as Claire, when using strict logic to solve a problem, she would at times accept things on face value when all the evidence pointed the other way.

But Rachel also thought of Claire as her best friend, and knew that Claire felt the same about her. In the beginning the psychiatrist in her had looked for overt actions of one sexual gender over the other, but the transition had been so gradual that there was no one point to put your finger on and say, 'this is where is started to change'. Who had once been Danny was now becoming Claire, and in a few weeks, if they survived, that same dual personality would have to reverse itself. The ramifications of that action were still to be felt. Pulling up a wicker chair Rachel sat next to Claire, who was lounging on the recliner and picked up some of the discarded issues. "How can anyone read this crap?" Rachel looked at some of the titles.

"Do me a favor and look very closely at any particular issue." Claire continued looking through the magazines. "Tell me if you notice anything really odd."

"You mean other than the titles and illustrations?" Rachel asked.

"Yes. Be more analytical of the issue itself."

Rachel looked at the cover of the issue she was holding. It was dated December 1991. There was a scene of aliens performing some kind of experiment on a scantily clad blonde girl with large breasts. The caption said 'Aliens probed her deeper than anyone ever had' under the illustration. The magazine had seven stories. There was a table of contents, a reader's page with questions about invasions and giant spiders in the desert of Africa, and some advertisements at the back. The magazine was fifty-eight pages long.

"I give up." Rachel tossed the magazine on the porch. "What am I looking for?"

Claire put down her issue and looked at her friend. "There are no issue numbers or volume numbers anywhere. Likewise there are no editors, publishers, contact information on how to subscribe, who prints this, or where." She watched Rachel pick the magazine back up off the porch. "Also there are no authors to any of the stories, and I did some phone calling this morning and none of the advertisers still exist. I called over a hundred of these numbers and none of them are working. You would think that at least one number in a hundred, spread out over thirty years, would still be active."

"You've gone through all the issues?" Rachel scanned another copy at her feet.

"Every one of these that you see here." Claire looked down the driveway. "No information at all about this magazine." Looking back at Rachel. "And I tried to find this magazine in the databanks. It's not listed in any library collection, bookseller inventory, or the Library of Congress. I don't even know where Claire got these."

"Other than that, did you find anything useful?" Rachel was getting hungry.

"Found a story about how Daryl Carter died." Claire got up, as if reading Rachel's mind, and started picking up the issues scattered around the lounge chair. "Also found an interesting story about the old mills where they said our folks died. Other than that, nothing new."

Rummaging around the fridge the two girls found some leftovers for lunch. Taking their food back on the front porch they started eating.

"Do you have those two stories you said were interesting?" Rachel pulled the pile of magazines closer to her on the floor.

"Gee, you mean you actually *want* to read something?" Claire passed the two issues to Rachel.

"You've been right so far, why chance fate." Rachel took the first one, which was called 'Wittlin" and started reading.

WHITTLIN'

"Jesus, I seen him."

Old Daryl staggered into the filling station white as a new blizzard. Ralph Marsted helped the old man into the empty chair and handed him a can of Blue Ribbon.

"Sweet Jesus, I tell ya, I seen him."

"Seen who?" Ralph's kid asked. Bill Marsted sat on a Pepsi soda case. He nestled his chin in his hands and tried to understand what Daryl was talking about.

"I seen Ned Carter!" Daryl was shaking so hard the beer was foaming out of the can onto his plaid work shirt.

"How many beers you had?" Ralph grabbed the beer away.

"I ain't had a beer since noon." Shakily he retrieved his can and emptied it.

"Daryl listen to me." Bill stood up. I know'd Ned for sixty years afore he died. You two was there when we buried him, let's see, eight, no nine years ago."

"You think I'm a old, crazy fool, don'tcha?" Daryl stood up, "but I seen him. Plain as day."

"We don't think you're crazy." Ralph kicked his heavy legs and work booted feet on the station desk. "Now tell us just what happened."

The old man sat back down. His face was back to its original color, a tanned, winter wind brown. He swept back his white hair and opened his frock.

"I was coming home from Mrs. Kelly's. She had me over for supper cuz it was my birthday and all. I'd had a beer or two at Marty's afore going so I was pretty dry after leaving Ethel's house and figured I'd walk back toward Marty's by the back road. When I passed the church I seen him sitting on the bench. He was below that sign that says 'Carter Falls Congregational Church' with his old knife he always had, whittlin' a piece of wood."

Daryl started shaking again.

"You sure it were Ned?" Ralph looked into Daryl's deep blue eyes.

"It were Ned a'right. He looked up when I was afore the church and I said 'Ned' and he smiled and waved his hand. I was so scaret I run up the road without looking back. This was the first place I come to with a light on.

Bill gave Daryl a ride home in the wrecker. He had to go through every room in the old man's house before Daryl would let him go.

"Bill, do me one thing." Daryl took hold of Bill's collar. "Look by the bench, please Bill. He was there. I knowed it."

Bill drove the old International down to the church. He felt foolish walking to the bench but old Ned had been known to do strange things up by that graveyard he farmed next to.

When he got to the bench he took out the heavy work beam and flashed it on the ground. The wind was howling something fierce but as he turned to leave, he looked under the bench. Reaching down he pulled a couple of wood chips from under the bench leg. His foot kicked something! It was an old buck knife. Turning it in his hand he saw the initials in the handle, NC.

Bill ran for the truck. He pulled a U turn right over Mr. Mapley's flower bed and headed for Daryl's. When he reached the house he left the truck in gear; it choked twice and stalled. He pounded on the door until his knuckles bled then kicked the door open. Running through the kitchen to the back of the house he reached the bedroom, stopped cold in his tracks and stared at the bed.

Daryl was propped up as though he had been reading. His eyes were open but they were past seeing. On his lap was a small cross, carved from an old piece of pine. Bill took his pulse but knew there would be none. Daryl had died, the way it looked, from sheer fright. It was then that he noticed the rocking chair by the wall. On the floor in front of it was a neat pile of wood shavings, as though someone had been whittling.

"Okay, that was weird." Rachel passed the issue back to Claire. "You have the other one handy?"

Claire handed another issue to Rachel and continued eating.

The story was more an article of a letter discovered at the Carter Fall's mills during some demolition work, in the seventies. The letter transcripted was supposedly written on parchment and stained with blood. Rachel doubted either of those, but read the letter anyway.

July 7, 1849

My dear son Albert;

Please accept this posthumous letter of explanation and apology with the love and caring that I write it. My body is hopefully laid in that ancient crypt so thoughtfully conceived by your great grand father Ezekial. I pray to God one last time that I be allowed to rest there more quietly in death than I ever did in life.

As to the events of my death I shall attempt a certain degree of fore shadowing while giving you some history of my past few months on this peaceful planet. As you know I was these last few years involved with a certain chemyst named Randolph Justin Baker who was instructing me in the ways of the Old Ones. These Old Ones had inhabited this planet before mankind was a slime of primordial ooze of the sea.

Utilizing incantations and noxious chemicals the learned man and I delved into the dark, forbidding past. Once last month we came very close to penetrating the blackened void that surrounded our goal. Doubling his efforts the man I grew to think of as a brother became maniacal. He worked day and night on his chemicals and potions. From somewhere he produced a molded and worm eaten leather bound volume of incantations in what he said was first century Aramaic.

With these new found tools we again peered into the depths beyond Hell. What I saw there last night I cannot hope to fully describe. The temple we stood before was greater than any building I have ever seen. The stone was of a black so intense as to swallow all light. Engraved upon it's front were letters similar to the ones in the book but these, upon seeing them, filled me with a dread that permeated to my vary marrow.

Quite suddenly and devoid of any sound a creature appeared before the alter. It was a great mass of a grayish colour with a worm like head and four-lizard type clawed feet. My companion stayed perfectly still during this but I cried out at the profane gestures performed by this devilish behemoth.

The creature turned quickly and uttered a single cry out of its' open oral cavity. The air was filled with a soul-wrenching odour too ghastly to describe in similarities and then it reached out and grabbed my poor fellow adventurer.

I admit freely to you and God that I should have tried to assist although I realize it would have been futile and my death would have been premature. I escaped somehow back to this room where I am sitting now.

Albert, my only flesh, I do not know what that thing was the tore poor Randolph limb from limb. I heard the bones snapping as I ran and thought I could almost experience the sucking of the internal organs from his still warm carcass. It has followed me to this world, or at least it is attempting to.

The very fabric of our time is being ripped apart as it gropes for me. The air is already oppressive and malodorous. There is nothing I can say to help you understand or defeat this if my death is not enough to return it to it's abysmal habitat.

Remember my son I love you and shall continue to battle this until my end. If you shall survive this bitter experience think not unkindly of me for I have paid the price of blindly searching for knowledge beyond where man should look.

Your devoted father,

Christian Anthony Carter

"That's got to be the craziest one of all." Rachel tossed the magazine back to Claire. "Where do people think this stuff up?"

"Reality can sometimes be stranger than fiction." Claire put the two magazines on the lounge cushion and tied the rest with some old string. "Jules Verne and H. G. Wells were thought great fictionist of their time, but now what they foresaw is commonplace. Who's to say this isn't accurate?"

"We can find out pretty quick." Rachel got up. "The gas station in the first story. Are you contending that it's the one in town?"

"It could be." Claire got up also and picked up the bundle off the porch. "The guy who owns it is named Bill Marsted. His father started the business years ago."

"Let me guess." Rachel walked inside. "His father's name was Ralph."

"Yea." Said Claire.

"I need to mail the package to Manny." Rachel returned. "Show me your, I mean, our home town. This place does have a post office, doesn't it?"

At two o'clock the two women were standing in front of the Carter Falls Post Office. Rachel had mailed the discs and papers to her ex roommate in Washington; certified. Director Rodriguez would get the package tomorrow afternoon by three and then would decide what best to do with it. For now they waited, again.

The town proper of Carter Falls is about six blocks. The one main street Centre Lane Road, runs from Route 153 north past the falls and the new golf course to the town of Madison. There is a second street, called Second Street, which runs parallel to Main Street for four blocks just west. Both streets cross the Ossipee River. Three other roads run into the town, or more properly, run out of the town; the northeaster, Cemetery Hill Road, crossing over the Saco River and going past the old textile mills and cemetery to dead end at the Carter Estate, Young's Road, which for some reason had all the apple orchards on it, goes from Centre Lane Road up Sweat Hill, to a logging road and then on to Highway 160 and then to Porter, Maine, and Cutter Road, leaving the town at a southeasterly direction, connecting to Route 25.

Rachel and Claire walked from the Post Office to the Sunoco at the corner. The sign was pitted from years of winter salt and the gas pumps were old hand crank types. A sign above the door identified the station as Ralph's Sunoco. Only one individual was in the small office when the girls entered. The man was about fifty with black hair and a bushy mustache. The Sunoco shirt he wore said Bill above the pocket. Claire grabbed a Moxie and a Diet Coke out of the cooler at one end and gave Bill a five-dollar bill from her skirt pocket.

"Hi Bill." Claire smiled at the man.

"Claire Daniels." Bill looked her up and down twice. "I haven't seen you in years. How've you been?"

"I'm doing better." Claire sat on a greasy stack of tires by the window. "Bill this is my friend Rachel, from Washington."

Bill took a long time looking at Rachel before he smiled again and said. "Nice to meet you Rachel. You've got a real famous friend here."

"Really." Rachel feigned interest. "How so?"

"Claire here is the only Ph.D. this town has ever had." Bill reached under the counter and held up a framed photo of the real Claire Daniels receiving her diploma, decked out in her cap and gown, the Governor of New Hampshire presenting it to her.

Bill looked at the photo. "You never told me the Governor presented you your Ph.D.." Rachel turned her back to Ralph and rolled her eyes to Claire.

"You forget some things when you get shot." Claire stated back. "Bill if I asked you this already, humor me, my memory is still a little shaky from the accident." Claire kicked her feet onto another set of tires, remembered she was in a skirt, and put them back on the floor. "Were you and your dad here the night Daryl Carter died?"

Bill dropped the photo on the floor where the glass shattered across the concrete. "I haven't thought of that night in years." Rachel helped the man pick up the bigger pieces and Claire found a broom and started sweeping the shards.

"Tell us about it, if you would, please." Rachel was about eight inches face to face with the shaking man. Claire thought if Rachel got any closer the two of them would be arrested or engaged.

Bill sat in the swivel chair behind the desk. Rachel took a position next to Claire on another set of tires.

"It was cold that night." Bill started slowly. "Daryl came in and said he saw Ned Carter in front of the church." Bill pointed down the street to the church. "Dad thought Daryl was crazy, but humored him and took him home. The next morning after Dad had helped the state police load the body into their car and take it to Conway he said something odd. He said that the dirt at the church had just been rotor tilled that morning. Standing in the bedroom, looking at the body in the bed, Dad looked down and saw dirty footprints: dirt from the churchyard. Dad's set entered the bedroom, but he said there was another set of footprints, starting at the bed and only going out. He never mentioned it to anyone else and I forgot it until just now. Funny how your memory plays tricks on you. Why the interest in Daryl?" Bill grabbed a Pabst from the cooler and opened it.

Claire thought of the story and shuddered slightly. It had the account right down to the beer. She thought for a moment and decided to try the truth. "I saw Daryl in the tunnels the other day."

"I'm not surprised." Bill drained his beer. "The Carter sisters still talk about him as if he's up and running around." Bill's eyes sort of glazed for a minute and then he snapped back to the present. "Dad believed until he died that Daryl saw Ned that night and that Ned came to the house to finish carving out the cross they found on the body."

Standing up Claire thanked the man for his help. Rachel smiled again at him as they left and he watched them from the front window walk back down the street to the post office where they parked the Porsche. Reaching behind the driver's seat Claire pulled out the tied stack of magazines and walked to the library.

"I have an idea." She said to Rachel.

Walking into the old building they saw Miss Carter on the main floor this time. She was shelving books across the back wall from a book cart. Seeing the two girls she crossed the main room and smiled.

"I'm done with these now." Claire put the stack of tied magazines on a table next to her. I have four others, however, that I'd like to keep for another week. Is that okay?" Claire was gambling that the real Claire had gotten the issues from somewhere in the library.

"You keep them as long as you like." Miss Carter picked up the stack and walked to a desk in the corner. Laying them in the center she returned to the girls. "Were they any help?"

"Yes ma'am, but I have a question." Claire sat down at the table. "I couldn't find any information about the issues. I know that magazines usually have an international number that keeps track of them. They also usually have some kind of contact information about publishers and the like. These didn't have anything."

"You're talking about what's called an ISSN. It's the identification number for all journal or magazine material." Rachel walked along the shelves looking at the titles. Miss Carter sat across from Claire. "We got the subscription as an anonymous gift." Miss Carter continued. "They show up from time to time. I always thought that they were from an independent printer who published the magazine as a hobby. Never could find the source. The cancellation is from Portland and the issues are always sent fourth class book rate."

"Miss Carter?" Rachel approached the old lady. "Your sister said something the other day about a restoration project, but I haven't seen anything that warrants restoration in here." Pointing to the shelves. "Some of these books look like they've never been opened."

"These books are for the tourists that use our library during the summer." The librarian stood up and motioned the two girls to follow her. She crossed the small room and entered a short hallway.

"I don't show this to people but since you two are Carters I think you should know what your legacy is." She opened a narrow door and stepped onto a rickety landing. "Watch your step, these stairs are probably as old as the town."

The three walked down a long flight of stairs and onto a granite-blocked floor.

"You're below the tunnels now." Miss Carter entered a brightly lit room. "This is the digitization project of Carter Falls."

Rachel and Claire stared at the expanse of the room. They could feel the controlled atmosphere being circulated through the ventilation system. The room was enclosed in glass and wood, probably one hundred feet long by fifty feet wide. At points throughout the room pillars of stone held up the ceiling. There were computers along the far wall and personal workstations at thirty different desks. Hundreds, if not thousands, of books were shelved here and there. Rachel counted nineteen people, mostly below the age of forty, working at different stations. She had enough knowledge of the process to identify some taking digital photos of the manuscripts, others working on the templates for the transferal, and others manipulating the data. Thinking of the ancient system of card catalogs and oak shelves above ground this room was like a science fiction movie where the evil genius tells the hero about ruling the world.

"What is it that you are doing?" Asked Claire.

"The Carter collection of metaphysical subjects is the most

extensive in the country." Miss Carter led the other two around the room. "Here we are putting all the knowledge accumulated through the years on digital disc and holographic chip." She struck some keys on a keyboard and a book appeared on a table in front of her. "This book can be not only read in the digital sense but can be viewed in the physical sense."

Turning to the girls she handed a book to the girls and ask one of them to place it on the table next to the holographic manuscript. Rachel took the book and laid it on the wooden worktable. The book fell through the table and struck the floor. Rachel picked the book up and handed it back to the librarian.

"The table is holographic also?" She asked.

"Yes" Hester was almost laughing. She tossed the book on a real desk behind her. "We keep the table up and running so we can import the images quicker. I thought it would be a fun experiment to see if you could see the difference. Our computers are state of the art in holographic imaging." Leading her charges back to the entrance she continued. "When we're finished here all the real books will be donated to the Special Collections Library at Brown University, to be housed next to the Special Collection of H. P. Lovecraft."

The three climbed the stairs back to the surface world. Claire and Rachel said good-bye to Miss Carter and walked back to the car. On the way Rachel turned back to look at the old building that housed so many secrets. Claire stopped in the middle of the street to wait for her friend as a piece of asphalt spit at her feet.

"Shooter." Cried Claire.

Rachel jumped behind a tree and Claire dove over the trunk of the Porsche. They both came up with pistols in their hands, scanning for signs of the sniper. Before either could call for backup they heard more gunfire up the hill to their right. Rachel's cell phone was ringing off the hook while they continued scanning the area, and answering it she called to Claire.

"The boys have a lone shooter pinned down behind the church." Rachel shouted to Claire. "Can you see anything?"

Claire looked through the trees on the far side of the street and up the hill to where Second Street passed. The Carter Falls Congregational Church was on the east side of the street poised on a great outcropping of stone, with a few trees at the top. From her view point she couldn't see anyone moving, but if a shooter was there, then he had a clean shot to most of the lower section of town, which took in the Post Office, Grocery Store, Sunoco station, and Library.

Working her way to the back of the Porsche she opened it and pulled out the floor mat. Beneath it were a number of firearms, one being a M1C Sniper Rifle, with an M82 Telescopic sight. Sighting the rifle on the hill Claire could see movement and the glare of what looked like a scope. Shouting back to Rachel she said.

"Who's on the hill?"

"Frick and Frack"

Looking back to the hill Claire could now see that the young girl that had been haunting their nights at the farmhouse held the rifle. She was holding a Winchester 30-30 with a small deer scope.

"Christ, it's the girl from the other night." Claire yelled across to Rachel.

"Can you get a shot from there?" Rachel asked.

"Are you kidding?" Claire returned. "With this thing I could count her nose hairs." Claire could now see the entire face of the girl. "I can put a bullet between her eyes any time."

"Then do it." Rachel was getting anxious.

"Tell whoever is south of the shooter to draw her fire. I want her up on one elbow so I can get a better shot at her." Claire steadied the rifle on the fender.

Rachel conveyed the instructions and called to Claire. "Frack says if she shoots him he's going to be real pissed."

"Tell him that if he gets shot, I'll apologize profusely." Claire readied for the shot.

"He says that's not much consolation, but get ready." Rachel watched the hill from her vantage point.

Frack fire a couple of rounds in front of the shooter and then moved into the open, affording the young girl a clear shot. The Butler girl turned to aim at the large target not more than two hundred feet away. As she swung her rifle around to get a shot Claire fired once. The heavy sniper round went through the stock of the Winchester, through the shoulder of the shooter and into the ground behind her. Dropping the rifle Frick was on her instantly and had her pinned to the ground while Frack picked up the weapon.

By the time the two agents brought the girl down the hill Sheriff Rogers was pulling up with all the lights and sirens going. He lumbered out of the cruiser and approached the five people clustered in the middle of the street.

"What the hell is going on?" John looked from one to another, trying to assess the situation.

"She tried to shoot them." Frick pointed to the two girls and passed the rifle to the sheriff.

Claire walked up to the young girl. "I told you I had nothing to do with your brother getting killed and you still tried to kill me." Claire back fisted the girl so hard in the face it spun her around and knocked her over. Before anyone else could react the red head, her face flushed with anger, picked the girl back up off the ground by the collars of her army jacket and slammed her against the tree that Rachel had hidden behind. "I could have put a bullet between your eyes." Claire shouted into the girls face. "Do you understand what dead means?"

Claire threw the girl back to the ground and walked away. "John," Claire said, "you can do whatever you want with her."

Frick went back up the hill to retrieve the SUV. Frack, Rachel and Claire watched as the sheriff put the girl in the back of his squad car and drove away, probably to the hospital in Conway.

"What brought you to town at just the right moment?" Rachel queried Frack.

"Mac pulled up some stuff on your library friend, Hester Carter, and sent us to get you. He said what he has doesn't make sense, so it's probably correct." The SUV stopped behind the Porsche. "When we pulled into town we saw the girl unloading a rifle from her truck and walk up the hill behind the library." He pointed to the back of the church. "We figured you were the target so we started to flank

136

her when you walked into range. The rest you know."

Claire grinned from ear to ear and lightly punched the older agent in the arm. "I'm glad she didn't shoot you. You're handy to have around."

All four laughed at that comment, the tension of the moment finally broken. Claire and Rachel got into the Porsche and the two men did the same with the SUV. A short drive later the four were in the farmhouse recounting the adventure to Mac and Myer.

"You had no intention of killing the girl did you?" Frack asked.

"No." Claire was adamant about unnecessary killing. She did not want to fall into the behavioral patterns of her cousin.

"You took a hell of a chance, though." Myer broke in. "Frack could have been killed."

"It was a chance that I hoped everyone would take." Claire was getting a headache. "I had a clear line of sight on the target. I could have dropped her at any time. I thought that if I had a little better view I could do what I did. If not the fall back would have been center mass." All the others understood the reference. Largest section of the body, the center of mass, is the sternum and heart. The power of the round would have exploded the girl's chest, killing her instantly.

Rubbing her eyes she asked what Mac and Myer had come up with while everyone was out playing.

"Your librarian is 98 years old." Mac was short and to the point. "The only reference I have on Hester Carter was that she was born, with her twin sister Hannah, in 1903, at the hospital in Kezar Falls, Maine. Their older brother Daryl was born in 1887.

"Are you certain of the dates?" Rachel couldn't accept the information.

"I told you it didn't make sense, but in this town that usually means it's accurate." Mac frowned at the others. "I have begun using reverse logic. If I look for something now I accept the farthest from reasonable and work from there, since the farthest from common sense is the closest to the truth." He looked at everyone else in the house. "Am I wrong?"

They all shook their heads in agreement.

While Claire took a hot bath to get rid of her headache, Rachel told the four others about the gas station and the computer room under the library. For technologically adept individuals the four men had a hard time accepting that there was state of the art digitization equipment in a town that believed in ghosts and demons.

"I think sometimes," Rachel said, "that this town keeps it's appearance of homey back woods Yankee for the tourists. There's more under the surface than meets the eye, but I just can't figure it out." They all moved to the living room. "Everyone knows what's going on, almost as it happens, yet I never see people around town, or driving through. Out of curiosity can someone pull me up a list of who lives in this town."

There was no communal dinner. Claire ate soup, Rachel a sandwich, Mac went out for Pizza at a little mom and pop place in Effingham, just over the river, and Frick and Frack munched on junk food.

Rachel got her list about nine that night. There were over four hundred residents listed in Carter Falls, Claire being one of them and the farmhouse being given as the address. Not surprisingly over seventy-five percent of the town had the last name of Carter. Pulling up the census data from 1990 Rachel could see that there were very few children in the town, the mean age of the residence being 51.4 years of age.

Claire had said that she wanted to go back to the tunnels in the morning and turned in early. The boys stayed up and worked or read. Rachel wondered if they had lives outside of the agency since they never talked about family, relatives or friends. She would have asked, but just didn't want to appear nosy. Instead she called it an early night and also turned in.

May 22, 2001, 2200 hours
U.S. Customs Checkpoint
Niagara Falls, Canada

Steve boarded the bus with the rest of the tourists. He had charted a seat to view the Falls from the United States side with a Canadian passport and driver's license. By midnight the group, numbering two hundred, reached their hotel and Steve had disappeared. By sunrise he was on Interstate 89 driving east to New Hampshire.

CHAPTER TEN

1000 hours, May 23, 2001
Route 153
Effingham, New Hampshire

Steve was glad he hadn't shaved since leaving the country two weeks ago. Looking in his rear view mirror not more than fifty feet back was one of the black SUV's from the farmhouse. Steve didn't like the idea that the agent was going to follow him all the way to town so he slowed down and pulled into a feed store. The black van roared past without giving the beat up truck a second look. After buying a beef jerky and an iced tea Steve continued on to his cottage on the hill.

1100 hours, May 23, 2001
Daniels Farmhouse
Carter Falls, New Hampshire

Mac pulled the SUV into the drive and got out. Frick was checking the oil in the other van and waved. When Mac entered the farmhouse the two girls and Frack were getting ready to leave. Before they could walk out the door, however, Mac dropped the bombshell that they had been waiting for.

"Steve's back in town." Mac threw the newspaper on a chair and carried the small bag of groceries into the kitchen.

Claire and Rachel were behind him instantly.

"How do you know?" Claire was first to ask.

"He was in front of me on the way back into town." Mac stored the produce. "Must have shit when he looked in the rearview and saw me pulling up behind him."

141

"You sure it was him?" Rachel worried that everyone was starting to look like the enemy.

"It was him." Reassured Mac. "I've seen the truck a couple of times around town and pulled the plates. He's been using it for about a month."

"And when were you going to tell us this?" Claire wasn't certain if she was pissed or pleased.

"When I was sure." Mac finished in the kitchen. "Now I'm sure."

"Good enough." Claire realized that the issue was resolved. It would do no good to get into it with her co-worker. He had done what he needed to do.

"We're heading for the tunnels. Get ready for tonight. Look's like we may have another visitor." Claire was out the door and into the van.

Carrying different equipment this time they entered the library and went back into the tunnels. Rachel thought at one point about the hidden room under their feet as they passed through the basement. She wondered what other rooms were hidden in this town.

At last the three were standing over the corpse of Kathy Robbins. Taking the heavy work beams from their packs they began scanning the cavern for other entrances or exits. The beams shot out from the three and penetrated the darkness. Working in sections the light identified three areas of the cavern that could possibly be a tunnel or additional cave. Claire took out some white engineer tape and some sticks. Using the sticks to hold the tape she and Rachel made directional markers from where they were standing to the three possible openings. This way they could retrace their steps if they got disoriented.

The first area they looked at was a shallow cave that had fallen into the main cavern. The rocks were strewn from what looked like a natural occurrence, and the small cave was at least as old as the larger one. The second area was just the way the light played against the stones. A small stream had broken through high on the wall and it made the stones darker than the rest of the wall.

The three adventurers hit pay dirt, however, with the third area.

The opening was half as big again as the tunnel they entered from. The dust on the floor was thick. If there had been footprints there they had been covered hundreds of years ago. Frack took a glow stick from his pack, broke it, and stuck it on the rock with some putty. Unlike the commercial glow sticks available in stores, these were special and would stay bright up to twenty days. With the marker to their backs and their lights to their fronts they began down the tunnel.

The distance gauge on Rachel's hip showed they had walked almost a mile when a breeze started blowing Claire's hair into her face. She brushed it aside and they kept walking until it happened again. Stopping the three could feel a draft against their backs. Moving more cautiously they continued, the lights scanning every inch of the tunnel floor and walls before anyone moved forward.

A few minutes later the lights showed a hole in the floor where the tunnel opened up into a small cave. The hole was about ten feet round, apparently either cut or blasted into the solid rock floor. There were no dirt or rock piles in the opening. Either what had been removed was in the hole or had been taken away. The pull of the draft was greater as they approached the hole. It wasn't enough to pull anything into it, but it was strong enough to make its presence known.

Frack again dug into his pack and pulled out a small flashlight and a balloon. Tying the ring of the light to a short section of string he placed the light on the ground and inflating the balloon from a gas canister in his hand watching as the balloon rose and then started to lift the light. Before the light cleared the ground he stopped and tied off the balloon.

"I learned this trick from my dad." He said, putting the gas tank back in his pack. "The balloon is full enough to keep the light from dropping too quickly, but not full enough to keep the light from not falling." He walked over to the hole, clipped a thin wire to the light ring and dropped the balloon over the edge. "This line is a thousand feet of mono filament nylon leader. It should give us an idea how deep the hole is."

The light fell steadily. In a few minutes the light was too far into the hole to be seen, yet the line kept paying out, and the balloon kept falling. Finally the line ran out and there was a tug at Frack's hip. "That's it." He said. "End of the line." He laughed at the pun.

"How deep is the hole?" Claire asked.

"No, you don't understand." Frack kept laughing. "That's the end of the line. The balloon stopped because the line is still attached to the spool."

Understanding Rachel asked. "Do you have another spool of line?"

"No." Frack said. "I never needed that much line before. Now what?"

"Cut the line." Claire reached into Rachel's pack and pulled four more stakes and some more white tape.

Frack let the spool go as Rachel and Claire roped off the hole with reflective tape. They took a break after that and then continued down the passageway. Each in their own way they wondered what could cause a hole to be over a thousand feet deep.

After walking in an upward direction the tunnel dead-ended in another half mile. To the naked eye it looked as though there had been a shaft at one point and been filled in, or had filled in on it's own, with dirt. Claire again went to Rachel's backpack and this time pulled out a small black box. Pulling up the antenna and pushing the single red button she laid it on the ground.

"We might as well go back home." She said. "This will give us a position when we get to the computer at the farmhouse."

They walked back down the tunnel, past the thousand-foot hole, past the still glowing chemical stick, through the great cavern and out the wooden door, which they locked from the outside. They exited the library building, this time with no one shooting at them and drove back to the farmhouse. Rachel marveled at how time seemed to slip away when they were in the tunnels. It seemed that no matter how long they were down there, it was always dark when they resurfaced. Perhaps time really does fly when one is having fun, but was this fun?

Back at the farmhouse Claire went straight to the global positioning software in the computer. When she finished inputting the information from the tracker she left in the cave she stood back and waited for the blue triangle to appear. With the house being represented by a green square the software could position the tracker anywhere within two hundred miles unless it was more than fifty feet below the surface. Using the largest scale for the maximum coverage she was disappointed to see just the green square.

The three unloaded the equipment and went back to look at the computer screen again. Still, they saw only the green square. Myer then thought to tell Rachel she had gotten a call from her ex roommate in Washington. The message was that the candy arrived this afternoon and her father ate it all before she got home from work. Rachel assumed that meant Manny had the data and was working on it since both he and his daughter hated candy.

After supper Rachel was sitting in front of the computer when she yelled at no one in particular. "What if the tracker is too close to the house?"

Everyone stopped what they were doing. Claire ran over to the computer swearing.

"I should have thought of that. Shit." She started punching keys. The map of the area began to get more detailed. What had been small lines for roads became thick black ones. Finally only the immediate property around the farm was showing on the screen. True to Rachel's intent the green square was sitting next to the blue triangle. Rachel pointed to the square and looked up at Claire.

"If this is where we are right now," she stuck her finger on the green square on the screen, "how far is this?" She moved her finger to the triangle.

Claire moved the mouse over to a chart on the left tool bar and clicked an icon.

"Seven feet that way." She pointed toward the living room.

Rachel walked into the living room about seven feet and stopped.

"So I'm over the tracker?" She started smiling.

"Damned tunnel really is in the basement." Mac screamed. The rest of the group headed for the basement door when the phone rang. Frick picked it up and answered. "Daniel's farm. Yes. Just a minute." He handed the phone to Claire with his hand over the mouthpiece. "Benjamin Franklin Carter."

Rachel couldn't tell if Claire was shaken, frightened, excited, or surprised. The redhead took the phone and began speaking. "This is Claire. Nice to hear from you too sir. Yes sir. Thank you. That would be very nice, yes. That's really too much trouble. I can have one of our friends drive us. If you insist. That would be fine. Certainly. Good night." She hung up the phone.

"Who was that?" Rachel inquired.

"That was the patriarch of Carter Falls." Claire leaned against the door jam. "He's invited you and I to dinner tomorrow night at his place. When I said one of the guys could drive he just passed it by and said he'd send his car. Said if we felt threatened we could bring our guns with us. He also asked if I would bring the key I found in the stream."

"Does everyone know everything around here?" Mac asked. "Why don't we just send the message out on drums next time?" The mention of drums made Rachel uneasy. "If we ask pretty please will this town make Avery and Levesque disappear?"

"I sometimes think it could." Claire returned. "Don't put anything past this town." But the comment was already lost to the rest of the group. Nothing was too far fetched to any of them anymore.

"Hey" Yelled Myers. "Let's go dig a hole in the ground."

The six went into the basement with shovels they retrieved from the attached tool shed. Standing approximately where she had on the floor above Rachel struck the shovel into the dirt and began to dig. The rest of the agents took up positions around her and started making holes of their own. At about two feet the four males struck stone. Claire was able to dig another few inches before she also was halted by rock. Only Rachel continued digging undisturbed.

The farmhouse, it appeared, had been built on a rock outcropping; the foundation lay directly on the bedrock. When Rachel took a break Frick replaced her and the hole progressed. In the stone had been cut a rectangular opening four feet by six feet. The shaft dropped directly into the earth with smooth sides and sharp corners. Someone, at some time in the past, had taken a lot of effort to cut this exit, or entrance, depending on how you approached the farm.

Frack was next in the hole. It was already eight feet deep and the dirt had to be handed up by rope and bucket, with Frack using a ladder. Mac and Myer went to the barn to get some rough hewn 2 x 12s to cover the hole when they finished, to keep people from falling in, or as Claire offered to keep things from falling out. At nine the group quit for the night. They were tired, hungry, and curious. Not understanding the severity of the winters in New Hampshire the men couldn't see the need for an access to the town area. Rachel had been a skier in her youth and understood snowfall, and Claire was a Yankee from birth.

That night the red dot reappeared. Everyone in the house knew it had to be Steve. Whether he knew and didn't care or didn't know he was being watched he stayed just out of sight of their cameras until the lights went out. At that he moved around the farmhouse to the driveway and then out to the street. The occupants of the farmhouse made certain he had easy access to anything he wanted to look at. They took notes as to what he came close to and what he avoided. In the morning the guys would casually check everything in Steve's path for traps and devices.

Meanwhile Claire and Rachel bathed and retired to Rachel's room. They sat in the dark and talked about what ever came up. They talked about the tunnels, the hole, the digging and finally the invitation to dinner tomorrow night. Rachel was the one to ask, since Claire seemed to know the answers.

"Tell me about this Carter guy we're having dinner with?" Rachel could only see the outline of Claire against the window.

"He was ancient when I was a kid." Claire said, her voice coming from the darkness. "He lives up Cemetery Hill Road, past the mills. The Carter house was built forever ago. I think it was the early 1700s. We used to say it was haunted, and now I'd not swear it wasn't. I don't know if he ever married or had kids. All we knew was he ran

147

the town from the hill."

"Can we ask the boys to look him up tomorrow?" Rachel snuggled up to her pillow.

"Yea." Claire got up to go to her room. "That would be a good idea."

Rachel sat on the bed for a long time after her friend went to sleep. She worried that this tunnel project was detracting from the real mission of Avery and Steve. As an agent she couldn't see how digging in the basement could prove important to the overall plan, however, as a Carter she was driven by the same desire that Claire seemed to have, find the answers to all the mysteries of the town.

She walked down stairs to the fridge for a glass of milk, and had just reached the kitchen when the first shots rang out in the yard. Dropping to the floor the black girl waited to hear breaking glass so she could decide which way to move and into which room, but no windows or doors were being hit. It was then that she realized the shots were actually firecrackers. Moving into the conference room she looked at the screen as the others filled into the room. Claire was the last one in when another bundle started.

"Now what?" She asked.

"Looks like fireworks on time detonators." Mac was in front of the monitor. "Our friend probably left them to see what our reaction would be." With the glow of the screen behind him he looked back at his boss. "What is our reaction?"

"None." Claire said flatly. "Let him think that we either don't care or didn't hear it. That should throw him off a little more." As she started to go back upstairs Claire stopped and turned back around. "What's the weather for the next two weeks?" She asked. "Also could whoever is on tonight check on Benjamin Franklin Carter for me? Planning session in the morning."

Claire dreamt all night. She was naked in a vast snowfield. All around her were huge monoliths and stone buildings, so large that she couldn't realize their height. Carved into many of the strange doorways were star shaped symbols and instead of steps there were ramps. As she moved through the landscape she could see her reflection in the ice and on very smooth metal plates that were inlaid in the walls. She was much older. Her breasts sagged and her hair was very long, windswept, and mostly gray. In her hand was the key that she had found earlier in the creek. Being drawn to a dark tunnel up a vast ramp she entered it and was entwined by great moist tentacles that began to squeeze the air from her. In the dim light she could see one red eye amidst a grouping of coarse hair. What looked like a mouth opened revealing yellow stained fangs. As the creature lunged for the girl with it's clawed hands she screamed and woke up sweating in bed.

Rachel was in the jungle. She was the same person as her earlier dreams, old, withered, naked and black. Around her were drummers of all races and colors. Some of the individuals farthest from the fire didn't even appear to be human, more of a humanoid shape with large ears and lidless soulful eyes. Her hands were covered in blood and in her left she held a long knife. As the music built to a crescendo she gyrated more and more about the fire and the drummers. There were three men tied to stakes at one end of the clearing bare to the waist and gagged. One was white with brown hair and blue eyes. The one in the middle was oriental, although the ethnicity could not be determined. His head was shaved and he had a long mustache and short beard. The last man was black; so black Rachel thought that if she put her hand to him it would pass through as though it were the night. His eyes were wide in fear and fought the hardest to escape.

Dancing faster she approached the three. Taking a grip of the brown hair of the first she pulled his head back, kissed him fully on the mouth and with one motion cut his throat. The crowds at the periphery chanted louder as the life ebbed from the body. She moved closer to the second man as he struggled to be free. She could taste the hot blood on her lips from where it erupted as she cut the throat of the oriental in a vicious swipe.

Now covered in blood from the two slaughters she approached the last victim. He thrashed at his binds but they held firm. Straddling his leg she appeared to be riding him, her legs wrapped around one of his. She kissed his face and neck slowly bringing the knife up to his throat. At the last moment she turned and then turning back in a wide arc almost severed the head from the body with her knife.

The fire blazed in an intense heatless flame. More dancers joined the fray and the ground began to vibrate under their feet. Rachel looked at the fire and saw something growing in the center. It was snake-like with a large head on a long neck. Where there should have been arms or legs were short-clawed appendages. Now towering over the women in the clearing it looked down with it's blood shot eyes and grasped Rachel by the waist. Before the creature could pull the black girl to its mouth she screamed and woke in a pool of sweat in her bed.

Myer dreamed of deserts. At first he thought that he was back in Arizona, where his grandparents had had a ranch, but the sand was too fine and the horizon was too far away. He was dressed in jeans and a tee shirt, his boots filling with sand at every step. Far on a hill he could see what looked like a stone building, but at this distance the edifice would have to be of immense size and shape. For what seemed like days he walked to the building, finally reaching it. The stone blocks that made up the structure were each taller than he. The doorway was of such size that three trucks could drive through at the same time and not be crowded. There were no windows that he could see and he didn't think he could walk around to look at another side without considerable effort.

As he stood there gazing into the darkness he felt a vibration under his feet. It was if the sand was running out in an hourglass. He began running wildly away from the structure but kept getting bogged down in the sand. Falling he was covered by a shadow from something that had emerged from the doorway. Before he could turn around to look he heard a scream and woke up with a start. From the floor above both girls were screaming in the night.

In different forms of dress, but each with a weapon in his hand, the four male agents rushed the two bedrooms on the top floor. Almost simultaneously they flicked on the lights to the hall and each bedroom. Claire was sitting up in bed her sheets wrapped around her waist tightly, her hair across her face and sweat dripping off her nose and nipples.

Rachel was lying outside the covers with her hands over her face. Her body was also covered in sweat, which made the naked flesh appear to be even darker and shinier than usual. With four men standing within ten feet of the two girls, neither one appeared concerned for their modesty, only their sanity.

"Are you all right?" Frick asked. He had never seen his friends like this and it bothered him, not the nudity, but the sweat, which meant that whatever they had been dreaming of had not been good.

Claire fell back on her pillow and said, panting. "Yea, just a really bad dream."

Rachel uncovered her face and said she was also okay, just shaken. She rose and without dressing walked to the bathroom for water.

"What time is it?" Claire looked at her clock. The sun was beginning to rise over the trees and the clock registered six forty three. "I guess it's time for breakfast, since I'm not going to sleep again today.

"Eggs." Rachel called from the hall. "Someone make eggs."

No one argued. Myer went to the kitchen, also not wanting to go back to sleep. Frick and Mac went back to bed and Frack resumed his turn at the monitoring equipment. Another day had started.

CHAPTER ELEVEN

Early Morning
May 24, 2001
Levesque House

Steve dreamed. He was standing above three bodies in a morgue. The one closest to him was Claire Daniels, his friend, enemy, lover, victim, and target. She was naked on the slab, the single exit wound of the machine pistol still red and open in the middle of her chest. Other than the wound she looked like she was sleeping.

The body farthest from his was his best childhood friend, Danny St. Claire. Danny was lying on the slab, the lower part of his body covered by a sheet. Three open wounds across his chest showed where Steve had shot him point blank. Steve thought that Danny looked restless, as though having a really bad dream, but he knew that couldn't be since he was dead. Steve wondered if the dead dreamt.

The body in the middle was Steve's. There were no apparent injuries. A sheet lay over his body with only his face showing. Walking to the first body he took Claire's hand and held it for a moment. Thinking to himself that soon he would add wounds to the living version of this girl he dropped the hand and arm and moved on. Passing his body he went to Danny's on the slab. He looked down at his friend for some time and then moved back to his own image on the table. As he approached his body the eyes opened and he jumped back in shock. At that moment a rooster crowed somewhere over the hill and he awoke. It was seven o'clock in the morning.

Steve went to the bank of television equipment and turned one of them on. The fuzzy screen showed the Daniel's farmhouse, already with lights on and activity. He would play the tape back to see what

153

time they started their routine and then make preparation for the assault, which had to come soon. He had business to attend to in other places and this project was taking just too much time. Even revenge had its limits.

By eight Claire, Myer, Frack and Rachel had eaten something and were ready to get down to business. Leaving Frick and Mac upstairs asleep the four met in the conference room and started the day session. Claire was her self today, calm, driven, focused. There was no little girl lost in her manner and no one in the room doubted who was in charge. She took a note pad from the table and sat at one of the console chairs, pad in front of her. Rachel was at her regular position on the couch, which now had been pulled closer to the tables and Myer was sitting next to Frack at the computers.

"First," started Claire, "let me have the status of last night."

Frack pulled out the night's log and began ticking off the events. "The fireworks ended when we went to bed. No one has been out to see the yard, but there doesn't appear to be anything else amiss, at least from our camera points." He turned the page. "It appears that while we were all upstairs this morning someone or something carried off the tracker from the tunnel. The computer registered that the tracker moved down the tunnel until it went off the scope. Nothing more on that at the moment." Another page turned. "I think you'll like this better, though." Frack turned on a small television set at his right and a blurred picture of the front of the farmhouse appeared. "I found static this morning when I ran a diagnostic on the cameras. Looks like Steve left this last night on his way down the drive." The picture was clear enough to make out all the detail of the front of the house.

"Before you ask." Frack put up his hand to Claire. "No. I did not find any other cameras on any other frequencies. It looks like this one is the only one."

Claire studied the image for a few minutes and then smiled. "Anything else?"

"Weather report says rain starting Saturday night and going through Sunday mid day. Real heavy by the sound of it." Frack turned yet another page on the log. "Finally your friend on the hill. As best I can figure he's about a hundred and sixteen years old. The house has been in the Carter family since it was built in 1698. The total square footage is estimated at over seven thousand and the out buildings spread for a mile in any direction. The estate owns thirteen square miles of forest and fields. There is no income listed to Mr. Carter directly but the IRS shows that he pays taxes on a combined net worth of 1.7 billion dollars, mostly held in gold and precious colored stones. The Carter trust also owns resort hotels in a dozen cities, a football team, and a chain of bookstores in Europe, Asia and the African continent that specializes in occult and metaphysical subjects. Up until the sixties he traveled extensively but has not left the country since sixty-seven. The postal people, however, report that he receives regular packages and letters from every continent on the planet and always signs for them personally when they are delivered to his house. He is the only patron in town that gets direct mail, everyone else using the mail boxes in town." Frack closed the log and waited.

Claire sat at the table and said nothing. She knew what had to be done and only needed to figure out where to start. Before she could talk, Mac and Frick entered the room. Tapping her pencil on the note pad now filled with sketches and notes she smiled again and looked at the other five in the room.

"Okay." She started. "Here's the game plan for the rest of the week." Everyone knew it was not going to be an easy time. "First I want the tunnel cleared as soon as possible. I know some of you wonder why this is so important and here it is. We need a way in and out of this place without being seen by the camera out front." Mac and Frick were lost at that one, but would have to catch up later. "Rachel, I want you to contact Avery, LeMay, Martino, she named another few high ranking directors of the agency, and tell them we have all the answers to what has been going on. Tell them I want to brief them on Monday morning in Washington. We expect to be out of here by Sunday afternoon, as soon as the storm passes and will be back at the office late that night." It was Rachel's turn to take notes.

"This will give Avery the next three nights to do something or risk us exposing his plot. My guess is the storm on Saturday is what he's going to use to cover his attack. Expect him anytime in the next three days." Claire nodded to her best friend and Rachel left the room to compose the messages.

"Next I want Mac and Frick to go to the library with shovels and lights. Get into the tunnels and start digging the basement opening from the bottom up. You've heard enough from the rest of us to be careful of the holes and misdirections. There can't be much more dirt to move, but be careful. Whatever moved the tracker may still be down there, and armed. Don't take any chances." The two men left the room and immediately began packing the SUV. In twenty minutes they were out the drive and on their way to the library.

"Myer. You and I will start on the tunnel at this end." Claire closed the pad. "I want it cleared today."

"What about me?" Frack sat at the computer.

"I haven't forgotten about you, believe me." Claire said. "I want a monitoring station in the basement by tonight. Also," Claire sat next to the agent and started drawing schematics on his pad, "I want it here." She pointed with her pencil to the paper. "I want it to do this and this" They talked for another few minutes in private. When they parted Frack knew what was expected of him and setting the monitors on automatic went about his business.

After Rachel sent her messages she joined the two in the basement. For the next two hours everyone took turns digging and lifting dirt out of the hole. Most of the basement by this time was filled with piles of dark soil mixed with lighter colored sand and gravel. It looked as if whoever filled in the hole used what ever was handy, taking a lot of it from the river bank and gardens out back.

A little after one Rachel drove her shovel into the dirt, heard a metallic sound and fell through into the tunnel below. They had broken through. In another few minutes they had the last of the dirt cleared and looked down a twenty-foot shaft to the tunnel floor below. Mac reported that it looked like a large snake had swallowed the tracker and crawled into the thousand-foot hole. Mac and Frick went back the way they came, locked the door behind them and drove back from the library to the farmhouse. For all intents and purposes no one except the six in the house knew the tunnel was opened and that was the way it was to be.

Claire and Myer pulled up the aluminum ladder and covered the hole with the planks. Whatever took the tracker was going to stay in the tunnels. By nightfall Frack had the computer equipment set up in the basement and covered with plastic to keep the dust off it. When needed it would be there. By two everyone was ready for lunch.

"What are you wearing tonight?" Claire queried Rachel.

"I have my black slacks and black jacket with the white shirt." Rachel finished her Diet Coke.

"What else do you have?" Claire put her dishes in the sink.

"I have my back up black slacks and black jacket with the white shirt." Rachel said.

"And what else?" Claire continued.

"I have the first black slacks…"

Claire cut her off before she could hear about the black jacket and white shirt. "You have nothing but service clothes?"

"No." Rachel looked at Claire like Claire had two heads. "Who knew I was going to live with a social diva for the summer?"

"Come with me." Claire took Rachel by the hand. "Auntie Claire will take care of you."

Passing two of the agents heading for their mid day naps Claire started looking in closets on the second floor. Not finding what she was looking for and with Rachel in tow she moved onto their floor and finally the attic. There in the corner was a dust-covered box with a handle on the top. Grabbing it and threading her way back down the stairs to the third floor she blew the dust off and set it up on her dressing table.

"I knew it was here somewhere." Claire said to no one in particular, although Rachel was still standing next to her and walked into Rachel's room. Claire rummaged in the closet and came out with a trash liner on a hanger.

"What a charming idea." Said Rachel. "I'm going to wear a trash liner. How novel."

"God." Claire looked at the sky. "I am surrounded by peasants." Turning to Rachel Claire said. "Black push up bra and G string panties, Oui?" Rachel said yes.

"Go put them on." Claire waved Rachel away. "And then back to my room."

Rachel was beyond asking questions. She found the Victoria Secret's push up bra in her drawer and slipped into her only pair of French cut black thong panties. Feeling like Naomi Campbell on the Italian runway she went back into Claire's room. There she found the red head with a pincushion on her left wrist and a Singer opened on the table.

With her hands on her hips Rachel stopped and with disbelief in every word said. "You're kidding? You sew too?"

Claire looked up and gave her customary enigmatic smile. "When I was at UNH I dated a costumer from the theatre department. It was the only way we could have time together. I got pretty good at it in four years, even after we split up." She ripped open the trash bag and pulled out a bright red ruffled shirt; ruffles down the front and on the cuffs. This was from my senior prom. Hideous isn't' it?" Rachel had to agree. "Put it on please."

The shirt fit just a little too tight in the bosom, which was what Claire had hoped for. "Bon." She said. "Now slip into this skirt of mine." Rachel swam in the black material.

"Cousin Claire must have been a size 16 when she wore this. It was after she and Steve broke up and she did nothing but eat and cry." The red headed seamstress started pinning the material into place. "I hated him for what he did but in retrospect it probably was the best choice at the time." Claire almost pinned skin to cloth. "Stop moving unless you want to be permanently attached to this."

After the pinning Claire cut and then sewed the material back together. When finished the skirt was cut to the hip on one side and flared at the hem. Looking at her creation Claire had to grin. She hadn't lost the touch even after all these years.

"Hair must be up." She said. "And you can use any of my gold."

Claire was satisfied.

"What are you wearing?" Rachel started taking off the nights wear.

"I have a Dolce & Gabbana dress," holding up a black scoop neck dress with bell sleeves and hem, "that I got after the shooting. No one has worn it yet. If you do gold I'll do silver." The two women laughed like schoolgirls and Rachel, now in just underwear threw herself onto the bed and laughed louder.

"I do enjoy being your friend at times." Rachel said.

"Only at times?" Claire shot the black girl a look.

"At times," Rachel returned, "you do make life difficult."

"But interesting." Concluded Claire.

By nightfall all naps had been taken, all applicable legs shaved, hairs put up, jewelry put on, and dresses donned. As if on cue a car pulled into the drive as the girls walked down the stairs onto the main floor of the farmhouse. Passing by the large mirror in the front foyer Claire marveled at how two grubby, dirty girls, playing in the sand at noon could turn into princesses by seven. Inwardly she was quite satisfied at her life at the moment, fairy tale though it was, but outwardly she kept her thoughts to herself, lest someone think she was losing more sanity than she currently had.

"Are you sure you don't need us to drive you there?" Mac asked.

"Are you kidding?" Frick shot in. "Did you see what they sent?"

Everyone went to the windows in the living room, where they could all see. Pulling up to the front door was a car from history.

"What is it?" Rachel asked.

"Fuck." Claire said under her breath. "He sent the Wraith."

The four men looked alternately from Claire to the sedan in the yard.

"It's a 1950 Rolls Royce Silver Wraith Saloon." Started Claire. "I've only heard of it. Carter bought the car new in 50 and had it shipped here from the factory in Derby England. When the Mount Washington Hotel was the epitome in luxury the Wraith was used to shuttle Carter and other dignitaries from the estate to the Hotel in Bretton Woods. I think my dad said that car has had nine different presidents and at least six kings and queens sitting in the back seat at one time or another. Gentlemen," finished Claire, "we are more than safe. There's nowhere on earth you could hide from Carter if you damaged that car."

Taking Rachel's arm in hers Claire walked to the door. "Ready to meet a legend?"

"Got the key to the kingdom?" Rachel asked back.

Patting her purse Claire grinned. "Right here." And out the door they went.

When the women approached the Rolls the driver was already out from behind the right hand steering wheel holding the back door open for them. The interior was what each expected. The burled mahogany, so typical of Rolls' of that time period was spotless. The leather was cream colored and immaculate. Even though the engine was running there was no noise once the doors were shut and the car glided out of the yard and through the night air as if on mist.

If anyone saw the car pass through town it was through curtain or blinds. There was no one on the streets. The women drove past the ruins of the mills where Claire's parents had been killed, past the town cemetery where all the Carters were buried and up the hill to the top. The road had once been a single lane dirt one, but in the ensuing years had been widened to allow two lanes of traffic. The trees that lined both sides of the road were tall, straight, and old. Claire remembered at one time being shown a Kings Pine not far from here. It was one of the pines that the shipbuilders in Portsmouth had identified as perfect for his majesties main mast of his war ships. It was the last one in the state if she remembered correctly. As the last of the light passed over Loon Mountain the car stopped at the entrance to the Carter Estate.

Rachel thought that museums were smaller than this house and probably not as expensive. The mansion had six floors, if one included the balcony at the top of the tower at the south end. Where Claire's house was a mix of styles through the years this house maintained one style throughout. Slate shingles on every roof showed their age with moss and green copper trim. The car stopped at the front entrance and the driver opened their door. Standing on the slate drive the two women looked like dolls in front of a great playhouse.

Before Claire could wonder what was next the doors opened and another servant, this one in tails, beckoned them into the main hall. Leading them through the downstairs they were escorted to a back library and into the presence of Benjamin Franklin Carter, patriarch of Carter Falls.

"Forgive me for not rising," the old man in a great black leather chair said, "but at my age energy is conserved more readily."

Claire approached the chair with Rachel right behind. She estimated the man to be well over ninety, although even she doubted the claim that he was one hundred and sixteen. There was a patch of snow-white hair on his forehead and age spots over most of his face. His eyes were deep blue but hidden and sunken from the years. The hands that extended from his heavy smoking coat were thin and yellowed, and his nails were dark and thick. Rachel figured his weight at one hundred twenty and his height at about sixty-eight inches.

In a soft voice Claire said. "Thank you very much for your invitation."

"It is I who thank you." Both women were surprised at the timber left in the old man's voice. Expecting frailty they could hear the strength still in the body. "You have done a service to me more than you could ever imagine." He motioned them closer to him. "If I may be so bold as to ask, did you bring the key?"

"Yes sir." Claire reached into her purse and for some reason handed the key to Mr. Carter. "What is so important about this key?"

The old man held the key for a few moments and then handed it back. "Let's eat, shall we? We can talk at dinner." Carter rose slowly and with short steps led the two women through a set of double doors to the dining room.

The room was vast. The table could probably seat fifty but tonight there were only three settings at one end. The elder Carter took the end seat and Rachel and Claire sat opposite each other. Food began to arrive. There were three soup tureens, ham and turkey slices, stuffing and dressing, vegetables and salads. Claire thought there was enough food here to feed twenty football players. A waiter poured wine from a bottle white with dust. The liquid was blood red and sweet to the taste. Rachel and Claire each took small portions of everything, not wanting to miss one of the greatest meals they probably would ever have.

"Please continue eating while I tell this story." Carter said between mouthfuls. "I think that by now, may I call you Claire and Rachel?" The girls nodded approval. "That by now each of you will believe what I am about to tell you.

"In the beginning before man, this planet was occupied by another greater species. They kept the dinosaurs as pets and traveled to the stars from whence they came. They built great cities in the Antarctic, the Gobi, the Sahara and Africa. These gods as some may call them possessed technology far superior to anything we have today. As wars took their toll of their numbers some of these gods escaped beneath the seas, others traveled to the far reaches of the galaxies and still others went between worlds. Finally the last few scientists of this race built a box to house all that was left of their science. This box was designed with five locks, since five was a number magic to these beings. The keys that fit these locks were made from star matter, collected in their travels, and matched the locks of the same material. Only the correct key could work the appropriate lock.

The keys were given to the remaining five scientists of this world, to be kept safe in the event their enemies won the war. Through the millennium these keys were passed down from being to being until the last remnants of this civilization crumbled into the dust of time. Only their cities remained, hidden, in far off lands and landscapes." Carter picked up his glass and drained the red liquid.

"Let me break here to explain why you two ladies are so important to all of this." He looked from one girl to the other. "Miss Jackson. I understand that you just recently learned of your Carter heritage. I regret that your family did not work out the way it was planned. Your ancestors are priestesses of Shudde Me'll. They are magic workers and soothsayers. For a thousand years they roamed the plains or Cthonia hidden deep in the forests of Central Africa. They prayed to the memory of the great gods of yore. When slavers began plying their trade to their region your family was captured and brought to this shore by way of the Caribbean. Patrick Charboneau, your ancestor, was not supposed to marry your many times removed grandmother. He was ordered to buy her and bring her here so she could marry one of the chosen Carters. Instead the upstart fell in love with her, and she him, and almost ruined the plan of centuries. It took another generation before we could set up a proper marriage where Elyse could be born. Then she marries the first man that passes through town and moves to Portland. I must admit you have kept many of us busy trying to figure how to get you back here."

Rachel tried to speak but couldn't find the words. She never liked being ordered to do anything, and now she discovered that people she didn't even know had arranged her entire birth and family tree for centuries.

Carter continued undistracted by the black girls thoughts. "Don't feel that we don't love you here in town." He said to Rachel. "You are family, and powerful family at that. There are great things in store for you after this nasty business is through." He looked back at Claire.

"And dear Professor Daniels." He smiled and Claire could see the teeth were yellowed and pitted. The gums receded from the teeth to give the canines a ferule appearance. "We thought we lost you also when that Levesque boy shot you and your cousin, but all worked out for the best. You may not realize it yet but you are now more than you could ever have been before. How we had to manipulate your parents and your aunt and uncle to marry and have a child each. Only your mother Denise," Claire realized that Carter knew who she really was. Denise was Danny's mother, not Claire's, "knew the truth since she was the direct line to the Carters. She really loved your father, but would have married Satan if so ordered. So now you both realize that who you are and why you are here now are not accidents in the grand scheme of chaos. You have both been chosen far in the past for things far in the future."

Carter held up his empty glass and the waiter filled it immediately.

Before he could put the crystal to his lips the desert was served. "Ah desert." Benjamin smiled obscenely. "I think that I eat meals just so I may enjoy desert."

There were four pies, apple, peach, pumpkin, which was out of season, and mince meat. An apple cobbler was placed in front of Claire and peach in front of Rachel. When all the wine glasses were filled, Carter began again.

"Back to the rest of the story. The first key I recovered from the Plains of Ur eighty years ago when I was a young man. I dug it from the ground myself at the base of the great temple to Hestus. Our family has had the box of the ancient gods for seven hundred years but the time had never been right to attempt recovery of the keys until this past century.

The second key came from the ice palace of Ithaqua deep in Antarctica. Sir Ernest Shackleton sent it to me from his second expedition that my father financed. I regret that what he found ultimately caused his death but it was a small price to pay for the key.

A geologist found the third key in the Sahara at an oasis by the base of a stone building said to be larger than any of the great pyramids of Giza. When I read an account of his experiences I realized that he had found the resting place of Nyogtha. He was all too anxious to part with the key after I named a sum. Unfortunately he never realized his wealth. He went mad shortly after relinquishing the key to me, ultimately hanging himself in his rooms in London one night.

The fourth key came from a short distance away from your original village in Africa, Miss Jackson. In the fifties a team of health officials from the United States came upon the city of the great apes, which were servants of Shudde Me'll. The soldiers protecting the health workers killed all the apes and ransacked the temples. The key was found by a nurse with the group and carried off just before an earthquake destroyed the entire area, killing everyone that remained. That nurse was one of our townsfolk and she brought the key home.

Finally we come to the key that you hold." He smiled again at Claire. "Your father found it in the ruins of the textile mills right here in town. He thought that it had been brought here by one of the many Native American tribes that worshipped in the area. He sent it to me the day your parents and their siblings were killed in the cave in. Somehow whomever he sent it with never reached this house and disappeared. I would imagine that since he was walking he slipped into the river and somehow drowned. In any event the key disappeared until you found it a few days ago. I imagine it took Hester quite a bit of will power not to show how important the key was when you showed it to her that day in the library. At that point we didn't know how much you knew or even whether you could be trusted with the knowledge. Hannah finally made the determination to tell you who and what you two were. In retrospect I feel she made the right choice."

Claire cleared her throat and looked at the elder Carter. "How did my parent die and where are they buried? I've tried for years to find out and no one will tell me."

"Your parents were killed in the tunnels under the old textile mill. Their bodies were never recovered, although that is something I have always regretted. The ground around the mills is so wet from the river and so fragile that the tunnels can't be trusted. We all tried to warn them to be careful but they were like you, driven when given a reason, and single minded. Does that help?" Carter looked back at the red head.

"Thank you, but why didn't anyone tell me that earlier?" Claire was trying not to cry about her parents.

"What would you have done? Dig in the ground with your hands until you found them or buried yourself next to them?" Carter was genuinely concerned. "You are far too important to risk dying in an accident."

"What is so damned important about me and this town?" Claire stood up and her fork fell to the floor.

"You'll know when it's time." Was all that the old man said.

Rising slowly from the table and with help from the butler who appeared at his right side, Carter made his way closer to Claire. "May I ask a small payment for this information and dinner?"

Realizing that to refuse might be dangerous considering the mental state of the man Claire said. "If I may."

"I would like to borrow your key tonight." He held out his bony hand.

Claire took the key back out of her purse but held it away from his outstretched hand. "I want to see the box."

Carter laughed. Rachel thought that she would never forget that laugh, part hysteria, part dementia and part humor. "If you promise not to touch it or the other keys." Turning to Rachel he added. "And you Miss Jackson would you also wish to see the box of the ancients?"

"I am here to follow Claire." Rachel said tying not to sound nervous.

"How far would you follow your friend?" Carter asked back.

"To Hell if necessary." Rachel returned.

"There are worse places on earth than that. Follow me please." The butler helped the old man down the hall and through a number of rooms until they stood in a small alcove, lined with books. "Now if you please, the key." Carter again offered his open palm.

Claire took the key and held it again.

"You feel the power don't you?" Carter stared almost to Claire's soul. "It vibrates in your hand, almost jumping to join the others."

Claire had to admit that there was a feeling in her hand and arm. It was as if the entire arm had fallen asleep and was only now awakening. Small pins and needles stabbed at her fingers and thumb. "If this key is so old, why does it look like just another key?"

Carter took the rusted key from Claire's hand. He walked over to a table and instructed the butler to remove the cloth covering it. There on the table was a large box probably four feet cubed of a golden colored metal or alloy unlike anything the two girls had ever seen. In front of the box were four keys, all shaped alike, but of differing hues of silver gray blue. Carter placed the last key next to the others and stood back.

"Because all keys were made to resemble these. These were the first keys in history, before locks were known on this planet." The new addition of the table began to vibrate and glow slightly. "The Egyptians modeled their locks and keys after these, as did every other civilization. Didn't you ever wonder why all locks work about the same?" Carter looked intently at the keys. "See," he shouted, "it knows it's own."

The rust fell off the key onto the tablecloth. The iron ring attached to the key crumbled to dust. After a few minutes the fifth key lay there shiny and new looking. Its color was the darkest of the five, but only if one looked closely.

"Shit." Was all that Rachel could utter.

"Ladies," the old man now started to appear nervous, "if you will excuse me for the night. I am intent on opening this box tonight after all these years of searching." Turning back to the girls he said. "I will send you your keepsake in the morning if all goes well. Again thank you for visiting."

The butler began leading the women out of the room when Rachel turned to the old man. "Sir," she asked, "when were you born?"

The old man looked at the black girl for a moment strangely. Finally he said "I was born on August 22nd 1879, right here in this house. Good night ladies."

The driver had the door to the Rolls open again when they exited the house. The ride back was as uneventful as the ride to the estate. At almost midnight the streets were empty and the lights at the farmhouse showed that the conference room was being used and someone was either in the kitchen or had left the light on, but other than that the house was dark.

When Rachel and Claire entered the house the four men barraged them with questions. It wasn't until the entire night had been recounted that everyone left behind was satisfied. It was then that Myer told Clair that Avery had sent orders by encrypted email.

"The four of us have been reassigned, effective immediately." Myer said. "We are to pack up all the equipment and report to Boston in the morning. I wrote back and said we couldn't be out until Saturday morning because of all the computer equipment we had here." Myer smiled with an evil grin. "Got an extra day out of the bastard. He just sent me a reply not more than twenty minutes ago. Said we could not stay past noon on Saturday because we were to be reassigned on

Saturday afternoon to a diplomatic mission overseas."

"Then why are you smiling so much?" Rachel knew something was up.

"I called my friend at assignments." Myer said. "There is no diplomatic mission overseas. We're being recalled just to get us out of the way."

"Because of that," interrupted Frick, "we thought we'd do some fast work ourselves. Tomorrow all four of us will take most of the equipment, with the exception of the new setup in the basement, and other places, and load them in the vans. I went to see Miss Carter, Hannah, and arranged for her nephew, who drove you two home the other night to meet us at the McDonalds in Laconia. He'll drive Chris and me back to the tunnels and lock us in after we pass through. Bob and Nathan, motioning to Frick and Frack, will continue in the vans to Boston and sign in. There's no reason to believe that Avery will be there to meet us since we're all betting the farm he'll be up here trying to kill you two."

Claire liked what she heard so far. "What about Steve?"

Myer looked back at Mac and then to Frick and Frack. It was Frick that stepped up to the plate. "I think that if you pack the Porsche Saturday morning, since Steve has the garage in view on his camera, he'll assume you're leaving also. He must be getting tired of waiting by now. The storm Saturday night should give him the cover to also come out of hiding." Frick looked like the Cheshire cat with his assessment of the situation.

Claire couldn't find anything wrong with the analysis. They talked about who was leaving what for a little while longer and then shut down for the night. No one was happy about what was expected in the next two days but the inevitable takes some getting used to at times.

CHAPTER TWELVE

0327 hours, 25 May 2001

The newspapers reported that a pocket of natural gas exploded, destroying a large country estate in northeastern New Hampshire at three twenty seven, Eastern Standard Time, May 25th, 2001. Other than local scientific reports and a flyby by WMUR out of Manchester two days later, no mention of the destruction escaped the area. It was another strange occurrence in an equally strange area of the state.

To the occupants of the farmhouse nine miles away it was the bombing of Hiroshima all over again. Although no windows were broken Claire and Rachel were both thrown from their beds onto the floor. The power was knocked out in the entire tri- county area for six hours and radio and television reception, with the exception of low-level frequencies, shut down until sunrise.

Flashlights in hand the six in the farmhouse made their way to the bottom floor. Claire pulled back a panel in the kitchen, threw a switch and heard the generator start. The computers came back on line and some of the lights burned dimly.

"What the hell was that?" Shouted Rachel, rubbing a spot on her head where she struck the bedside table.

"Reports are coming in now." Frack was at the computer. "Seismic out of Portland says an earthquake of, no fucking way, it says 7.4, hit nine miles from us at the top of," he pointed back toward the Carter mansion, "that mountain."

Claire ran up the stairs. "Everyone, get dressed. I want two of you to stay here and watch the perimeter, everyone else grab your weapons and badges."

Five minutes later the two SUV's raced out of the drive headed through town and up to the Carter estate. What had been a tree lined drive was a battlefield. The vans switched to four-wheel drive and had to climb over felled trees and limbs in the road. At one point just before they reached the adjoining fields of the estate they had to winch a tree out of the road that had to be two feet in diameter. It took both vehicles to move it. Finally they broke into the opening and stopped. The high beams of the vans lit the top of the hill. What Rachel and Claire had seen a few hours earlier, the mansion, the barn, the outbuildings, the fields of newly planted corn, were all gone. There was nothing on the hill but rubble. They drove slowly over tiny pieces of wood, tile, plaster, slate, and all the other things that make a house a house. No piece was attached to any other piece and nothing was over eighteen inches in length or width.

Claire parked her SUV in front of where the doors had been and stepped out. With search beams in hand the four scanned the area for life. Walking to the edge of the foundation Frick looked into the hole that had been the basement. It was half filled with shavings the size of wood chips from an industrial shredder. They continued their search until finally the state police cruisers arrived about five. Holding their NSA badges over their heads in the approaching headlights they greeted and then briefed the local authorities.

By seven, with the sunrise, the damage could finally be appreciated. Claire commandeered a state police chopper and got an aerial view of the destruction. The epicenter of the blast had been the house. For what looked like two miles in any direction the debris was scattered evenly. Trees were blown down in a circular pattern, all pointing away from the blast. There was nothing standing on the entire mountaintop, no tree, building, vehicle, nothing.

Clouds were forming when the four climbed into the two vans and drove back to the farmhouse. There was nothing that could be done. Whatever old man Carter had done with those keys and box had been wrong. Just before she walked into the house she remembered what it reminded her of. There must have once been another set of keys and another box. Someone in Siberia must have thought as Benjamin Carter had, that man could harness the forces of the ancients. The photo she remembered was the reported meteorite that struck the area of Tunguska Siberia on June 30th, 1908.

During the remaining morning hours the four men packed or moved the equipment in the conference room. It had been decided that Mac and Myer would stay at the farmhouse and that Frick and Frack would go to Boston and report in. The two that were remaining gave their pass cards to Frick. When the time came he would swipe his and theirs to make the computers on Comm Ave believe that all four were back in the Bay Area.

Frick finished his work upstairs. Claire had given very specific instructions on how she planned the next couple days. If it all worked, then by Sunday the black SUV's would return and pick up the remaining equipment and personnel. If it failed then another set of SUV's would make the drive from Boston to recover the bodies and what was left of the equipment. Either way all hard discs were wiped clean before they were moved to the basement and no floppy discs were left. If all failed there would be nothing to benefit the victor, whomever that may be.

Watching the television screen from the basement the agents made certain that Steve saw everything being packed and moved. They needed him to understand that this was his only chance. By lunch the boxes were all packed in the vans, some of them empty in the event anyone counted how many boxes went into the house earlier in the month.

With a light mist falling, Claire went to the garage behind the house and fired up the farm truck. Rachel had never seen the vehicle but when it pulled into the front yard she was impressed. The truck was an immaculate 1979 Dodge Warlock 4X4. There was chrome everywhere and a bank of spotlights across the heavy silver roll bar over the cab. Claire entered the house by the front door as Rachel met her at the landing.

"Is this another one of your projects?" Rachel asked.

"Naw." Claire took off her jacket. "My dad and uncle built it for duck hunting and working the property. It was supposed to be used for hauling brush, hay, you know, everything. By the time they finished it they kept it covered in the garage and bought an old Chevy Silverado. I'm going to clean up and go see Ms Carter. I think it's time to find out what happened last night."

"You think she'd know?" Rachel queried.

"Hell she knows everything else." Claire went upstairs.

Steve heard the blast along with everyone else in town. He got to the monitor in the living room in time to see the vans pull away and head down the drive. Later that morning as the first reports of the explosion were being broadcast over the radio he saw the vans return. What ever had happened on the mountain he surmised was attributable to the occupants of the farmhouse. Their target or targets must have been inside the old mansion. Steve gave the six credit. He understood the importance of the Carter estate from when he used to visit with the cousins in the summer. To take out the wealthiest man in New Hampshire must have been a great kick.

As he watched the house through the day he saw what he was supposed to see: the boxes and suitcases being loaded in the two vans. The assignment completed the four men were going back to, wherever. If this was truly the end of the mission then he may have already waited too long. He couldn't do anything but wait now and hope for a break.

Claire and Rachel drove down to town through the light rain. Claire worried that the storm would pass too quickly and they talked about moving up the timetable. When they reached Hannah's house the heavy front door was open and they could see lights on through the glassed in screen door. Before they could knock, however, the old lady was there to great the girls with a tray of brownies.

"Do you cook all the time?" Rachel asked, taking an offered brownie as she entered the house.

"At my age, dear," Ms Carter said smiling, "there isn't much else to do but cook and eat."

Claire joined her friend on the large couch with a brownie in hand. She didn't know how to approach the subject so she took the direct route but first she had a more pressing problem.

"You know about the plan tomorrow to have your nephew meet my friends in Laconia and bring two of them back here?"

"Yes. They came by last night. Such nice boys." Ms Carter passed the tray of brownies to Claire.

"Would it be possible to make the exchange tonight about eleven? I'm afraid the weather may turn bad tonight." Claire didn't want to give away too much.

"Of course." The older Carter smiled sweetly. "I'll have him there at eleven. Anything else?"

Claire thought for a moment before asking.

"Ms Carter?" She started. "Do you know what happened last night?"

"My, my." Hannah looked at the two in what seemed like mock surprise. "Why would an old lady like me know what the fine and mighty up on the hill do in their pretty mansions?"

"Because I think you know everything that goes on around here, and if I may say, I believe that this entire town keeps its look like a well groomed garden, nothing ever out of place, for those that come to visit." Claire finished her brownie and waited.

Hannah's demeanor seemed to change at that. She put down the small piece of brownie she had been playing with and looked at the two girls opposite her. She was no longer smiling and there was a serious business look to her face. When she spoke it was determined and no longer had the kindly grandmother tone she maintained.

"You are certainly good at what you do." She said. "I told Benjamin you would be harder to fool than the others." Hannah again put up her hand to stop questions from either girl. "There have been others here, Carters all, but from other parts of the family. We had at one time or other hoped that they would be strong enough to take control or at least understand what was going on but they were ignorant sheep. They thought that being a Carter was just a family name on the map. They never understood the power and responsibility that came with it."

The old woman took a deep breath and continued. "Your parents knew, all four of them. We had planned on both of you, you and your cousin, being able to continue the work and keep this town safe but that reckless foolish young man spoiled it. Now we have you, dear, and I told Benjamin and Hester when I first met you that you were going to prove to be the one. That's why I warned him not to start on the box without your help, but Gods help us all he was a stubborn one. Had to try to open it before it was time."

Ms. Carter stopped for a moment to catch her breath. "We have power. We know things that most of the world has forgotten or would like to forget. Some of our kin have used this knowledge to try to educate the masses but have failed. Others have simply gone mad. Now I will give you the chance to either join the mad ones or to succeed."

Claire and Rachel felt the hairs on their necks rise up. Even though it was cool in the house both of the girls were sweating and Rachel's tank top stuck to her skin

Still the old lady continued talking. "Everything Benjamin told you last night is real: the story of the Gods, the war, the keys, the box. I imagine by now you have both been having dreams." The two women nodded yes. "There is genetic memory in all of us passed down from one generation to another. That memory escapes into your subconscious at times and you dream. What you saw happened eons ago. The world was less structured then and more chaotic. The Gods were closer to the surface. What we do is monitor their activity. We report to those government agencies responsible for internal security where and when the likelihood of another contact will take place. Most of the work was done up on the hill, or actually under it, in other tunnels that Benjamin kept. He acted as the security guard, so to speak, for the world, but he was getting old and wanted to find the answer to the box before he died. It was going to be his legacy to the world. Now the box and the keys are gone, at least for a while, and we have to rebuild."

"I still don't know what that has to do with me." Claire broke in.

"Or me." Rachel chimed.

"If you survive the weekend you'll be very rich but very busy young women." Hannah stood up. "Yesterday morning Benjamin signed papers making you two the directors of the Carter trust. You won't be paid much, however, I think that Benjamin received about sixty million a year, but you'll be able to see the digitization project completed, and restore the observation equipment that keeps the planet safe. Monday if you're still alive, come visit. I'll make supper and we can eat on the porch. I hear the weather will clear by the morning at the latest."

"Ma'am," Rachel could barely get the words out, " if you know all this why don't you help us stay alive?"

Ushering the girls out the front door the old women went back to being the kindly grandmother. "That would take all the chance out of life." She smiled at them. "What fun would that be?"

Claire had one more question and pressing the point she asked. "You all maintain your lifestyle by choice, not by financial restrictions, correct?"

Hannah laughed a long time at that. Finally she answered. "Every Carter in town is richer than anyone could imagine. Anyone who isn't a Carter, but who has lived here for enough generations is also taken care of. You're right about the garden, but it's more like a museum. We are a living display." And with that she closed the front door.

"Sixty million a year?" Rachel said when the two got into the truck. "Was she kidding?"

"I doubt if that woman has ever told a joke in her life." Claire drove back up the road. "But remember we have to live to collect it, and then only if we're willing to play guardian to an entire planet."

"You can't tell me you believe all that?" Rachel was stunned.

"And you can't tell me you don't." Claire was clear in her words.

When they reached the farmhouse the rain was coming down hard. The four in the house had hunkered down in the parlor with a fire going. They listened to the update of the plan and had to agree. No matter what happened this weekend the weather was going to be a factor. Frick and Frack loaded the last of their clothing into one of the vans. Mac and Myer loaded two empty and two full suitcases into the other and prepared to leave for Laconia. They would be back in town by midnight and should be in the basement an hour later. They had already left lights and tools at the tunnel door when they went to see Hannah the previous evening.

Claire grabbed a suitcase from the closet. Rachel filled her duffle bag with the dirty laundry and threw it down the stairs. With the men being as obvious as possible without looking suspicious in the front yard they helped Rachel and Claire begin packing the Porsche under the side shed. With darkness the vehicles looked ready for a long trip and the trap was set. From time to time each of them had looked at the others on the small television screen in the basement, making certain that the image showed what they wanted to show. For all intents and purposes the six in the house were leaving, some sooner than others, but all within the next day or two.

At eight that night the two SUV's pulled out of the drive. Each man had hugged each woman good-bye before leaving. The two girls waved from the front porch and then went into the house. From Steve's living room the scene was convincing. The men were out of the way, and now he was free to act. Before he missed his chance he would have to get there tonight and finish the job. The weather was still only a light rain, but the clouds covered the waning moon adequately for his purpose.

Claire and Rachel had a late supper and then pulled all the blinds closed. In the morning they would draw the few storm shutters around the back of the house closest to the tree line and put up the plywood sheets across the side windows. The only windows that didn't have covers were the ones under the porch, since a storm strong enough to take out those windows would have already ripped off the porch.

The girls kept the lights on throughout the house. From time to time they would show themselves at one window or another, making sure that they were in sight of the camera in front. When one would pass by an open window the other would be in the basement looking for heat signatures. With the storm Steve could almost walk over one of the sensors before it would register and they hoped that if he came they would have adequate time to react.

As soon as the four men left the farm Rachel went to her room and put on the three Kevlar tee shirts. They fit very tightly and she had to put in push up pads to make it look like she was wearing just a regular shirt. Claire had taken off her bra and made sure that the buttons on her blouse were just barely held on by a few threads. She wanted to be able to pull the blouse open easily when the time came.

Frack had done his work well. The house was wired for sound, all going to the basement. Nowhere in the farmhouse could one go without their words or steps sounding on tape. All the carpet runners had been removed so that the wood floors resonated with each step. Also, the heat sensors that surrounded the property were on all floors. Mac or Myer could monitor who was where in real time. There was a heat monitor screen on the third floor that was wireless. Claire or Rachel could carry it around and sweep room to room if necessary. Finally each girl had a receiver/transmitter fitted to her ear. With their hair down it was invisible to the naked eye. If the need arose and both women were killed then Mac and or Myer could eliminate whoever did the shooting by keying into the scene by the transmitter still active on the dead agent and the remaining heat signatures.

The two men came through the floor of the farmhouse just at one. They reported that the trip was uneventful: no one following them either way. Claire instructed them to lay the planking over the hole, cover the wood with a tarp she found in the barn and then fill in the hole with dirt. There would be no entrance through the basement. If anyone came to visit it would be through the front, side or back doors, or in the event of an all out assault, then through a window.

Steve watched the last light go out a little after two. He packed his tools and left his rental by two thirty. He had cut a path through one of the stands of trees and around two fields to be able to cross the road just north of the farmhouse. When he got there, however, he stopped in his tracks, the night scopes he wore casting a dim green light around his face. Across the opening to the front of the farmhouse and just into the woods he saw someone else. The individual was very tall and looked equally thin. He was standing behind a large tree watching the house with a pair of binoculars. Steve sat in the wet brush and waited. If this was another guard that the girls had working for them, he was new. None of the others were this tall or thin. Not sure what to do he waited for the other man to make a move.

Avery never saw Steve. He had arrived just as the two vans were pulling out of the drive. Not certain whether the agents would return he took up a position that afforded a good view of the house and waited. In the morning he would log into the security system in Boston from his laptop and check to see if the four had signed in. There was time tomorrow night to kill the two girls and blame that idiot Levesque. He thought to himself that he should have just traded sanctuary to a third world assassin for the lives of the two in the house. It would have been easier but at the time didn't seem necessary. He laughed to himself when he thought of how the easy things end up being the most difficult in the end.

The rain continued through the night. Claire and Rachel slept soundly on the third floor. Mac and Myer took turns sleeping on the cot in the basement. They registered the position of Avery, although they didn't know which he was, as soon as they arrived. Steve had managed to stop just beyond the sensors and for the night had remained unnoticed. Just before sunrise, the heat signature disappeared from the scope. They had made it through another night.

Avery walked out of the woods at sun up. He uncovered his truck down the road and off on a logging trail. He drove back to his motel room in Long Sands, on Ossipee Lake. Tomorrow night he would act. For now he wanted a hot shower and some sleep.

Steve watched the tall man leave the woods. It was too late to make his move so he worked his way back to his house. No matter who it was in the woods tomorrow night would be the night. He would add one more death, the guy in the woods, to the list. Just don't let them leave today he thought as he drifted off to sleep.

CHAPTER THIRTEEN

27 May, 2001

Steve only slept a few hours. When he awoke he checked on the tape of what he had missed. Nothing had moved since he left the farmhouse. For the remainder of the day he packed his clothing and essential items. He would drive out of town in the morning, never to return. There was something about this town that had always bothered him but he could never put his finger on it. It was as if people watched him for no reason. These ignorant narrow-minded peasants could rot in their backwoods town for all he cared. Tomorrow he'd be back in civilization, enjoying the rewards of his labors, and looking forward to more of them.

Avery slept until noon. He checked his email and made some phone calls on his cell. Content that the four male agents on the case had indeed checked in to the NSA building on Commonwealth Avenue in Boston he put them out of his mind. There were now only the two in the farmhouse to take care of tonight. He thought that Levesque was still in England and regretted that. The fool had failed up to this point to kill the women and he had a rental house not more than a mile from the farmhouse.

Mac and Myer took turns at the console all day. They listened to the noises of the house and accustomed themselves to who sounded like what. Claire walked heavier than Rachel did, even barefooted, which they had each girl do as a test. Claire also usually wore sandals and Rachel was in sneakers when not in uniform. Claire spent a lot of time in the third floor bathroom, drawing water, letting it run out, and walking from there to her room and back. She had not told the boys in the basement what Frack had set up and they wondered if this plan was as good as it sounded.

The rain continued through the afternoon and the horizon started getting dark around five. Rachel and Claire had put up the winter shutters in the back and on the sides of the house. Rachel moved the padded chaise lounge chair that had been at the corner of the porch to in front of the picture window. At one point she went into the flower garden in front of the house and picked up something that she had deliberately dropped a few minutes earlier. At that point, with her back shielding the camera image she pulled a small cordless screwdriver from her jacket and removed all but the two top screws holding the railing in place. Pocketing the screws she went back into the house.

Claire cleaned her Glock 9mm and two other pistols and placed them strategically around the house. Rachel did the same to her side arm and another spare that she had brought from the city. Each of them could get to a pistol within twenty seconds if necessary yet none of them were obvious in the house.

At six the girls joined Mac and Myer in the basement for the final meeting of the night. Claire ate a small salad and Rachel had a banana. Mac had made himself a sandwich the size of a tank. It had ham, salami, turkey, two kinds of cheese, a thick slab of onion, bread and butter pickles, Miracle Whip and Guldens Spicy Brown Mustard. Washing it down with water he had that contented look that one sees at fine gourmet restaurants. Myer on the other hand had a cold can of Chunky Beef Stew. None of them could understand how the others could eat what they did. So much for diversity.

Avery left his motel room after nine. He packed the CZ-52 in his shoulder holster, put the silencer in his pocket with an extra clip of shells, and climbed into his truck. Satisfied that no one would expect him he drove to the logging road and walked to the tree by the side of the house.

Steve arrived in the brush shortly before Avery walked up. He had taken the same position as last night fully expecting the individual across the yard to do the same. Seeing the tall man and being careful not to give himself away with the lightning flashing above he maneuvered to a better position, closer to the house. From his new vantagepoint he could see the front and one side of the farm to include the attached shed and mudroom door. Scanning the area he didn't see any other guards, but when he looked back across the yard the man by the tree was gone. He crouched in the thick brush and waited. The lights in the house showed through the curtains in the living room. He could see a figure moving back and forth from time to time but couldn't make out if it was Claire or that bitch watchdog.

While Steve was moving to a better spot by the mudroom entrance, Avery had worked his way around the back of the house and under the eaves of the back porch. From there he was close enough to touch the back door, up three stairs. He knew from visiting the house in the spring before Danny had been released that the inner door of the porch led to the kitchen and then through a hall into either the dining room or the front living room. There were still lights on in the kitchen and other rooms and he waited there in the rain, thunderclaps above him, for the girls to go to bed.

Mac and Myer in the basement, warm and dry, watched the two approach the house. When one signature was close to the mudroom and the other at the back door Mac whispered into the mic.

"We have two bogeys in the wind."

Claire and Rachel had been sitting in the dining room playing cards. Rachel was the first to answer. "Roger base. On the move."

Claire chimed in a moment later. "I copy base." She said softly. "Going to take a bath. Switch to auxiliary power."

The lightning was directly over the farmhouse now. Rachel went to the conference room, turned on a single light, sat down on a chair and waited. She had put the three Kevlar shirts on again with the same push up pads and over that had put on a thin cotton work shirt, unbuttoned. Looking at her she appeared to be wearing a white tee shirt and open blouse with jeans. Claire turned off the lights in the dining room and walked upstairs to the third floor. She closed the curtain to the shower and turned on the water. The cold water hit the plastic with an almost tinny sound. Stripping to panties she pinned a large towel around her waist and made it look as if it were tied. She then took the Glock, laid it on two bath towels, put two more towels over it and laid it on the sink. Finally wrapping her dry hair in another towel she sat on the closed toilet lid and watched the portable sensor screen.

Myer watched the external sensor screen while Mac watched the internal one. Rachel had a tracking device in her pocket that glowed yellow on the screen. Claire had one in the folds of her towel that showed blue. The two bodies outside were still bright red.

"This is base, no movement outside. We have you both on screen." Mac said into each girl's ear.

"Base, I'm going to kill the power on the next flash. Good luck." Claire reached over to a small kill switch mounted on the side of a little black box. With this switch she could shut off all power to the house except her bedroom.

"I'm ready when I get the word." Said Rachel to the rest of the group.

The flash came with a shuddering clap of thunder. Claire's thumb flipped the switch and the house went black. Myer watched the red dot at the back of the house move to the door. At the same time the dot at the side of the house worked itself to the mudroom door and stopped. Rachel listened intently in the conference room, waiting for her cue to move.

Meanwhile Mac kept up a running commentary on movement. "We have one coming in the back door." He switched his attention to a micro camera mounted on the back porch hidden in a broom. From the television screen he could see the shape of a very tall individual coming into the covered area of the porch. "Back door is Avery." He said. "I say again we have Avery at the back door."

Rachel stood up and walked to the doorway of the conference room. She heard the back door open and the footsteps of the tall man walk into the kitchen. Picking up the book that she had placed on the end table by the doorway she threw it on the floor and yelled.

"Shit." The bottom floor resounded with her voice and Mac pulled his earphones away from his ears in the basement. "Claire is that you in the kitchen?" She walked into the hall slowly, watching the changes of darkness in the kitchen move. "I have a candle in the living room, I'll get it." She walked to the living room and to the coffee table by the front picture window.

"Avery is in the doorway between the hall and the living room. Right behind you." The black girl heard the voice in her ear. Rachel reached down and picked up an electric match next to a large pillar candle on the table. Just before striking it Mac came back on and said that Steve was coming in the mudroom door.

The match flared and the candle gave limited light in the large room. Rachel looked up and stared at the tall man holding a silenced pistol in his right hand. She dropped the match and ran for her pistol under the end pillow on the love seat. Avery fired and the first shot struck Rachel in the back below the right shoulder pushing her forward. The second shot struck her in the center of her back and she went through the single pane glass window. Before falling onto the chaise lounge and off the porch into the flowerbed she was struck again in the left ribs.

Avery walked over to the window and looked out but couldn't see anything past the broken railing of the porch. He heard a door far above him and then a voice.

"Rachel was that you?" Claire shouted from the top of the stairs. "I've got a candle going in the bathroom. I'm going to take a shower. Grab a coke and I'll meet you in my room in ten."

Avery cocked his head towards the voice. This was going to be too easy. Walk into the bathroom and shoot Danny before he can react. Moving through the dark house he started up the stairs.

Steve watched the shooting from behind the bar in the kitchen. He saw the tall man fire; he saw Rachel thrown through the window and in the dim light saw the material of her shirt rip as the shots struck home. He heard Claire's voice from above and watched the tall man move to the hallway and then the stairs. With his silencer firmly attached to his pistol he closed the gap between he and Avery in four quick steps. Before Avery could take two steps up the stairs Steve shot him once in the back, through the heart. The tall man fell to his knees and in falling backwards knocked Steve off his feet and onto the floor in the hall. Instantly Steve was back up and ready to fire again when he realized that the tall man was dead. Making certain to only step on the outside of the stairs, since old stairs always creaked in the center, he climbed the stairs to the third floor.

"This is base." Mac's voice came through Claire's earpiece. "Steve is heading your way. Avery is not moving in the hall and his heat signature is fading. Best guess scenario: he's dead."

Claire stood behind the wall of the linen closet in the bathroom and waited. By the light on the monitor two feet away on the toilet seat she could see Steve walk up the stairs to the second floor, search it, and then continue to the third. When he stopped at the bathroom door she breathed slowly and quietly and steadied her backup pistol, aiming at the door. She had thought of killing him at that point but she had things she still needed to know and dead he couldn't tell her. She'd let him live.

He moved past the door and into her bedroom. From the position she estimated that he was standing in the middle of the room in front of her rocking chair. She had left one candle burning in the room so he could find it easily and wouldn't fall over anything. When she was sure he was staying put she shut off the water and picked up the pile of towels. Supporting them on her left hand and holding the Glock in her right deep in the furry fabric she held them at chest level and walked into her room.

Steve was standing there when she entered, holding his pistol in his left hand, pointed at her.

"Hello Steve." She said, dropping the towels to reveal her gun. "I've been expecting you for some time." Carefully so as not to disturb the standoff she flipped the light switch on the wall and the lights flared in her room.

Claire stood in the doorway bathed in light. The towel on her head was intact and the one around her waist was still there. Her exposed breasts showed the three evenly spaced scars from the machine pistol. Holding the gun in a firm but comfortable grip she looked at her oldest friend, and deadliest enemy.

Steve looked at the red head, moved his eyes from her head to her feet, back, and focused on her chest. A smile slowly crept across his face and he lowered his pistol.

"Bravo." He said. "I would never have guessed that Danny was the one that survived. He stood there and fully comprehended the transformation. "You could have fooled your own mother, Danny-boy. You got me, take me in."

"What makes you think I won't kill you right here?" Claire never flinched in her attention. She knew too well that Steve could kill her if given a chance in less time than it would take her to pull her trigger.

"Danny." Steve said, and with the two men in the basement listening. "You never could shoot anyone in cold blood. Not like Claire. I think she lived for causing pain."

"Tell me something old friend." Claire spit out the last two words. "What happened to you? You were so good and so loyal."

Steve looked old. "People change, loyalties change, and you get tired." His shoulders sagged a little. "I met someone, fell in love, got married. Her name was Anna. She worked for the Czechs. We were together for five years." His face twisted by hate. "Then your cousin killed her. Shot her in the back." He straightened up a little. "After that all I wanted was revenge. Now I see I got it after all."

Claire stayed where she was. "One more question." She said.

"Anything Danny-boy. I never could refuse you." Steve looked contented.

"What happened to your finger?"

Slowly, so as not to cause the red head to fire, Steve held up his right hand. "When I got ready to quit the agency and go into private practice I needed help. The payment I made to show I wasn't going to go back to sniping was to give the Bosnians my trigger finger. I cut it off the night they took me in with my survival knife. Hurt like hell, but you know about pain, don't ya, Danny. You've also had your share recently." He put his hand back to his side, his left still holding the pistol.

"Now what?" Claire asked.

"Now you take me in." Steve tossed the pistol on the bed. "I know enough to keep the agency busy for years. Then I get a bank account and a trip somewhere safe from all the countries I've turned on."

"I have a better idea." Claire steadied her grip on the pistol. "How about this? I shoot you right here and we end it."

Steve started laughing. "Danny, "he said through the spasms, "you could never just shoot me. We both know that so why even think about it?"

The first shot took the laughing man in the sternum. Before he could register that he'd been shot four more rounds struck within three inches of the first. Danny's oldest and dearest friend who he had grown up with and loved like a brother fell over the rocking chair and crumpled onto the old throw rug in front of the glass doors to the balcony. He never heard the final words that would have prepared him for his death.

"Danny's dead." Claire said flatly.

EPILOG

1700 hours, 31 August 2001
Daniels farmhouse

For those that have never been to New Hampshire in the late summer the heat can take you by surprise. In August it can hit one hundred with little to no breeze, making the sweat pour off your body like a salty shower. Today was such a day, hot, humid from an early morning rain, and not a cloud or breeze to be found.

Claire stood on the porch and leaned on the railing that Rachel had fallen through. She was dressed in the shortest cotton skirt she had and a bright yellow bikini top that just barely covered her nipples. Her hair hung limply to her forehead and she wiped the sweat off her nose from time to time. The only relief she received was from the iced Moxie bottle in her hand, the cold beads of water on the outside, slightly chilling her hand.

In the yard was her blue Porsche sitting next to a 1989 silver Porsche 959. It had taken Rachel two months to get the feds to approve the car for road use. Since Porsche had never offered this model to the Highway Safety Commission for crash test, there had only been 250 of them made, they were illegal to import or drive in the states. The Carter trust had maneuvered the government to allow this single one.

Claire turned her gaze to look at the chaise lounge, now back at the end of the porch. Lying on it in a white bikini bottom and no top was Rachel Jackson. The Kevlar shirts had done their job, however, the black girl had sustained six broken ribs from the impact of the shots. She had also sprained her left wrist and right ankle when she dove out the front window and rolled into the flowerbed. Now, completely healed, she sat sweating, and looking for comfort.

187

Unfortunately for both girls the farmhouse, although having four fireplaces and two furnaces, had no air conditioning.

Claire thought of the last few months since the night Avery and Levesque died inside. True to her word Ms. Carter had supper that Monday. Rachel was bandaged and on crutches but the two girls, and the four males, Frick and Frack returning from Boston on Sunday afternoon, had eating in the formal dining room in Hannah's town house. Also at the meal were Hester, Hannah's sister, and a bevy of accountants and lawyers, all Carters.

Claire and Rachel soon realized that the Carter foundation was run by these men, and that as directors, which they accepted, the two women's role would be policy setting, face time, and research. They turned down the sixty million per year that Benjamin had been given, instead agreeing on a checkbook that would never run dry. Neither girl could envision spending more than a few million a year. The rest of the money was to be used to rebuild the Carter mansion, open the tunnels, and continue the work as before.

Claire asked the agency to release her and Rachel on permanent leave of absence in lieu of resignation. The assignment was quickly approved and the two remained active members of the agency, on assignment as deemed necessary by the director. Rachel requested, if approved by those concerned, that that the four men that had seen them through thick and thin be assigned permanently to the Carter project. This also done, the Carter trust purchased four houses by the new golf course for the men. Burns, who still answered to Frick, brought his wife and five children up to New Hampshire the next weekend and they settled into the town's life quickly. The other three bachelors spent time at Frick's house.

Claire thought about the route her life had taken in the past year. Someday she would have to write it all down, but no one would believe it. When her stomach growled she called to Rachel.

"I feel like seafood tonight." She saw Rachel smile. "Sound good to you?"

Rachel got up off the lounge. "Only if I drive."

Claire looked at the 959 again. She never thought she'd admit it but driving in the silver beast made her think that some cars really do go too fast.

Wrinkling her nose slightly and smiling she wiped the red bangs from her eyes and said. "Deal"

Walking past her best friend and long lost relative Rachel poked Claire in the ribs with her elbow. "You still have great tits." She laughed.

"Yea." Claire said with a wry smile. "I think I'll keep them."

Printed in the United States
966400001B

9 781592 864355